"Run, Finnley! G... growled out the w....

The intruder suddenly turned in her direction and aimed his gun at her. Gunfire blasted the apartment. Finnley dropped her phone and darkness fell again. Had she been shot? She felt no pain. She searched for her cell and found it. Turned on the light.

Caine rammed into the intruder who had almost made it to her, and once again, the two fought. He must have knocked the gun out of the man's hand or else Finnley would be dead.

She should do what he said and run, and maybe that would draw the attacker away from Caine. And to her? She couldn't fight him off. She found the will to do what she had to do. The strength. The man had Caine in a headlock.

She grabbed the gun and aimed it. "Stop or I'll shoot!"

Elizabeth Goddard is the award-winning author of more than thirty novels and novellas. A 2011 Carol Award winner, she was a double finalist in the 2016 Daphne du Maurier Award for Excellence in Mystery/Suspense and a 2016 Carol Award finalist. Elizabeth graduated with a computer science degree and worked in high-level software sales before retiring to write full-time.

Books by Elizabeth Goddard

Love Inspired Suspense

Honor Protection Specialists

High-Risk Rescue
Perilous Security Detail
Deadly Sabotage
Suspicious Homicide

Mount Shasta Secrets

Deadly Evidence
Covert Cover-Up
Taken in the Night
High Stakes Escape

Visit the Author Profile page at LoveInspired.com for more titles.

Be not afraid, only believe.
—*Mark* 5:36

To my Lord and Savior, Jesus Christ

Suspicious Homicide

ELIZABETH GODDARD

LOVE INSPIRED SUSPENSE
INSPIRATIONAL ROMANCE

LOVE INSPIRED® SUSPENSE

INSPIRATIONAL ROMANCE

Recycling programs for this product may not exist in your area.

ISBN-13: 978-1-335-59818-9

Suspicious Homicide

Love Inspired
22 Adelaide St. West, 41st Floor
Toronto, Ontario M5H 4E3, Canada
www.LoveInspired.com

Printed in Lithuania

MIX
Paper | Supporting responsible forestry
FSC® C021394

ONE

Grief lashed at Finnley Wilbanks's heart while rain pelted the windshield. The wipers worked overtime as dusk deepened. She hadn't intended to be driving this road in the dark. She hadn't intended a lot of things.

Life had taken an unexpected turn.

Dad was dead. Gone.

Murdered.

Nobody believed her on the *murdered* part.

Nobody as in Devault County Sheriff Tammy Henderson. Apparently, the coroner agreed with the sheriff.

Maneuvering the curvy mountain road that led away from Mount Rainier required all of Finnley's focus, but honestly, she was only giving it half of her attention. Her thoughts were scattered. The rest of her mind relived the last few days. She'd thought that coming up to view the mountain—specifically the Emmons Glacier, where Dad began his climb to the summit every year with Greg Jones—would give her relief and… perspective.

Oh, Dad!

Finnley had always been too afraid of heights to make that climb with him. Even the mountain roads scared her. But today—in her grief—she faced those roads.

Why hadn't she faced her fears earlier and hiked to the summit every year with him?

Dad, if only I'd known you'd leave me so early, I would have gone with you.

But no one knew when their last moment on this earth would be. She had so many regrets. She longed for a redo of the past. But that's not how life worked.

It didn't help that she had no one around to share her deepest thoughts. Her two best friends had found jobs in the city, and their attempts to meet once a year to catch up had failed lately. Finnley had a few loose friendships in town, but no one she would call close. And she didn't want to draw anyone else into this horrific drama.

She'd taken the drive, hoping nature could be her therapist. Instead of finding peace on this drive, she'd only grown angrier at Sheriff Henderson's declaration.

"Finnley, honey, you've got to accept the truth. We all loved him. I can't think of one person who would want him dead. Can you? He was a quiet and compassionate man. Let him rest in peace. Let his death be with dignity."

Dignity?

There was no way that her father could have shot himself. He had never owned a gun, and they'd planned a trip together. Finnley would not believe it. He'd bought them tickets for a cruise, and that's all he could talk about. Dad was a man who was excited for the future. They were supposed to be leaving on the cruise in a couple of weeks.

Tell me how that adds up to a gunshot to the head, Sheriff!

Oh Lord...help me. I'm crushed inside. I don't know how to get past this horror to find the truth.

To get justice for my father.

Finnley swiped at her eyes. The tears had surged again at the worst possible time. The rain and wind pounded her small sedan and buffeted it against the side of the road and a dangerously sharp drop. She corrected course and focused one hundred percent on the road. She couldn't get justice if she was dead too.

The rain eased enough that she was able to slow down the windshield wipers, and pressure eased in her chest. She hadn't realized how tense she'd become as a result of the sudden storm on a dangerous mountain road, along with her grief and rage.

Dad didn't kill himself!

Bright lights from behind told her a car was approaching a little too fast for comfort, and reflexively, Finnley slowed her own car to let it pass so she could drive safely at her own pace.

The vehicle came up behind her, but instead of passing, the driver inched closer as if to force her to increase speed.

"Really?" *Just pass me already.*

In the growing darkness, hands gripped tightly on the steering wheel, she focused on the road and was relieved when trees began to line the edge of the road to her right. At least now, if she went off the road, she'd go into the trees instead of dropping hundreds of feet. Of course, running into the trees could still be deadly.

The rain had slowed, and the wind had decreased. Now all she wanted was to get home and crawl into bed and pray for God to give her peace.

The car sped around her to the right. She would be relieved at the maneuver, except they were passing her on a big switchback—a curve in the road with a warning sign that distinctly warned against passing.

What an idiot!

Their car bumped the side of hers.

What?

"What are you doing? Get on your side of the road!" Finnley ground her teeth and slowed to let the car pass, but it slowed with her. Panic settled in her chest.

What is going on?

Fear ignited, and her heart rate spiked.

The car rammed her vehicle on the side again. Now she got it. This was intentional. Someone was trying to run her off the road.

Why?

This couldn't be happening.

Determination gripped her. Finnley wouldn't let them end her. She corrected course and rammed *her* car back into the attacking vehicle.

There. How do you like that? Two can play this game!

She accelerated and the vehicle tried to catch up. Finnley sped around the mountain, focusing on the road and not on the fact that she was probably still seven or eight thousand feet above the town of Emmons along the Mount Rainier scenic-view drive. Either way, driving like a maniac or letting those people take her off the road, she was in *lethal danger*. Fear threatened to strangle her.

Oh God. Oh God…please save me!

Who wants me dead? The same person who killed Dad?

It had to be. If only she was brave enough to pull over and get out and face them. But she had no weapon or protection. She would work to remedy that in the future, but she had to survive first. The trees had fallen away again, and all she could see was darkness to her right.

The car giving chase caught up on a switchback and rear-ended Finnley's vehicle. Her car started spinning, and Finnley screamed as she lost control.

I'm going to die!

Lord, please don't let me die!

The car crashed through the guardrail so forcefully that it went right through. The airbags went off, cushioning her, but she waited for the impact that would take her life. Squeezing her eyes shut, she prayed hard as the car rolled and rolled and rolled. Nausea erupted in her gut.

Pressing her hands against the roof of the cab, she screamed, her mind filled with fear and the unthinkable while her heart prayed for protection. The rolls slowly stopped, and the car rested upside down.

She gasped for breath, sucking in air.

I'm still alive?

Her chest ached from where her seat belt and the airbag had held her in place as the vehicle rolled. Obviously, the mountain had shifted to a gentler slope and not a dead drop.

She could figure that out later. Right now...

I must get out of here. What if they come down to finish the job?

Gasping, heart pounding, she unstrapped the buckle and knocked the rest of the glass out of her window. Finnley crawled out. She was making too much noise. She stilled. Got quiet. Listened. Her car lights were still on and illuminated the area around her.

Glancing up above, she made out two people slowly coming down the incline. To help her?

Or to kill her?

The tree line started up again below her on the slope a few yards away from where her vehicle had stopped rolling. Fortunately, she'd gone off the road in a small valley. While she wanted to wait for help, she couldn't take the chance that the two figures approaching intended her harm. She got up and limped around to the far side of her vehicle, reached through the broken glass and snagged her cell. She was in a dead zone, but her cell would ping, and searchers could find her that way.

She maneuvered deeper into the pitch-black woods. The rain started up again. She couldn't see without using the flashlight on her phone and hoped it wouldn't draw her attackers' attention. But maybe she was far enough into the woods now.

The wind blew hard, the tree trunks clacking together around her. Finnley hunkered next to a rocky outcropping beneath a naturally formed overhang. It was a modest shelter in the storm.

Thank you, Lord, for the small things.

She hugged herself and shivered in the cold mountain night. An hour later, no one had come for her. On the one hand, it was good the people who'd run her off the road hadn't found her, but she could die out here on the chilly wet night in these higher elevations.

A flashlight beam shined through the woods. She stiffened, fearing they were still pursuing her.

"Finnley? Finnley Wilbanks!"

She recognized the voice of one of the Devault County deputies. Her body stiff and aching, she slowly stood from where she'd been hiding.

The deputy—an older stocky man—ambled forward to where she hid in the small alcove. "We got a call that a car went off the road. I couldn't believe it when I found your vehicle. Thank the Lord you're okay. What happened?"

"I'm freezing. Can we just go?"

"Absolutely. I've called for a crew to come get your vehicle, but that won't happen until tomorrow. Do you need to get anything out of it?"

"My purse."

At her vehicle, the deputy shined the light around inside her car and then grabbed her bag and handed it over. They hiked the rest of the way up the hill, and she practically fell into the seat of his county vehicle. He handed her a blanket and cranked up the heat.

"I'll take you home, Finnley, but can you give me a statement now? What happened?"

"Someone tried to kill me, that's what."

Unfortunately, instead of outrage that someone would try to kill her, she saw pity in his eyes. He didn't believe her. He probably thought that grief, heartbreak and stress had her desperately believing that her father had been murdered.

I'm utterly alone.

Caine cleared his throat as he entered the kitchen. Maybe Ayden and his new wife, Hannah, would get a clue that he was here. Because right now, they were entirely too caught up in a kiss.

He reached for the fridge and opened it to look inside. Were they out of Dr Pepper already? He could feel Ayden's glare on his back.

To his way of thinking, office romance—office couples—were not the best idea. Having someone you loved working with you could be too distracting. And Ayden was proving his point. On the other side of that, office romances were distracting to Caine because he had sworn off all romance. He didn't want to be reminded that all his siblings—Ayden, Brett and Everly—had found "the one."

Oh, good. He found one last Dr. Pepper in the back. He took the soda from the fridge and popped the top. Ayden gave him a look as if he shouldn't be interrupting.

"You said you had a new assignment for me." Caine took another swig. "Well, I'm here to work."

Hannah pushed Ayden away with a smile. "Caine's right." She left them in the kitchen, giving Ayden a wink on the way out.

"Are you sure this is such a good idea?" Caine gave his brother a challenging stare.

"Hannah has a business degree and experience. She can help us grow. Why would I hire anyone else when she's qualified?" Ayden arched a brow, his tone incredulous as he exited the kitchen.

He'd give his brother a few minutes in his office to clear his head, and he'd savor the peace and quiet while he had it.

He was chugging his soda when Brett moseyed into Honor Protection Specialists with Kinsley.

"Hey, Caine." She smiled. "How are you?"

She was kind and sweet and smart. Brett deserved someone like that, so why was Caine irritated? "I'm fine. What's up?"

"I'm stealing Brett for the rest of the afternoon. Would you let Ayden know?" Her arms were entangled with Brett's.

"Is that right?" Caine crushed his can and tossed it into the recycling bin.

"Yeah, we need to look at wedding venues." Brett only had eyes for Kinsley. "It's better to ask forgiveness than permission."

Whatever. "Have fun. I'll let him know."

Brett led Kinsley out of the kitchen.

If Caine saw Everly and Sawyer cuddling next, he might just be sick. But nope. Everly was on the computer when he passed her massive office—which was really just the main computer room. She was their resource for all things IT and did their intelligence gathering.

Ayden was married and his other two siblings were engaged.

And Caine was alone.

By choice.

He'd fallen for someone in Italy while he was stationed in the army there, and the woman he'd loved died. After that, he'd decided to focus on his work and any nieces and nephews that entered this world thanks to his siblings. But all this office-romance business reminded him of what he'd lost.

He entered Ayden's office to find a petite woman with a khaki jacket over jeans and hiking boots standing there. She was small and had big brown eyes and soft curly black bangs that framed highly intelligent but grief-filled eyes. There wasn't a lick of makeup on her face. She had a scratch along her forehead and a sprinkle of freckles across her nose and cheeks. She looked young and innocent, but her soft pink lips were pursed with determination.

He realized he was taking in entirely too many details, but then again, he was trained to remember the details. But…he wasn't looking at her for his job. Staring at her like an idiot, he couldn't find his tongue.

Where are you, Ayden?

This must be the client. *Obviously*, she was a client or a prospective client. Caine found his composure and stepped forward, thrusting his hand out. "I'm Caine Honor. You must be…"

"Finnley Wilbanks. Ayden told me to wait here."

The man himself entered the room and rushed around his desk. He glanced between them. "I see you've already met. Finnley have a seat."

Finnley sat, and Caine got a whiff of citrusy shampoo or perfume. He tried to ignore that it made him happy.

Ridiculous.

He took the seat next to her. Ayden handed off a folder to him, and he opened it and quickly skimmed the case file.

"Finnley, I'm assigning Caine to work with you. He's a part of our team and also my brother. I trust him with my life, and I trust him with yours."

"Wait." She glanced between Ayden and Caine. "First, I was referred to *you*, not your brother. And secondly, I'm not hiring protection. I'm hiring you to find out who killed my father."

"I understand," Ayden said, "but after reading about the road incident, I think it's prudent for you to include the protection detail we offer. As for me, my caseload is full. I'm already committed and can't take on another client personally. But Caine is available and—" Ayden gave a teasing smirk "—he is every bit as skilled as I am."

Finnley frowned deeply, and her soft and innocent expression turned hard. Severe. That surprised Caine. She sat up taller. "Look, I've already filled out paperwork to purchase a gun, and I signed up for a training course."

Caine held his breath for a moment and shared a look with Ayden. "Miss Wilbanks, if someone is after you, there's more to protection than simply owning a gun, especially if someone is intentionally trying to harm you."

"Please, call me Finnley."

"Okay, Finnley," Caine said. "How about you let us—me— work with you for a few days and see how it goes." Maybe not the words Ayden would have used, but Caine needed to know that he could work with Finnley too. Would she listen to him?

He couldn't experience another failure, even if the situation with Sophie wasn't remotely similar to this one. Regardless, a trial run was a good idea.

There was something about Finnley… Something that set warning signals off in his head.

He'd only just met her, but she somehow managed to make him feel like she was looking at his deepest, darkest secrets. She was seeing places he didn't want anyone else to see. And he was drowning in those eyes. He was not in the mood for this particular battle.

Yeah…maybe he couldn't work with Finnley, after all. He flicked his gaze to Ayden and hoped his brother—the one who trusted Caine with his life—could read his mind now and see that Caine was the one who needed saving today.

TWO

Finnley tried to assess Caine, but he was hard to read.

"I have to think about that."

A trial run, was it?

She wasn't sure she liked being pressured into a protection detail. The room suddenly felt like it was growing smaller. These two strangers stared at her, waiting for answers. She'd invited them into her private life.

What had she been thinking? Sure, she needed help if she was going to get answers, but she hadn't considered the protection side of things. And now that she was considering it—a little—she wasn't sure she liked the fact that this guy would be protecting her. He made her nervous, but oddly not in a bad way. Maybe a good way, whatever that meant. She wasn't making sense, even to herself.

She'd gotten her liberal arts degree at the local college and worked with Dad in his little shop of papers, or rather his vintage stationery shop. She enjoyed her job and her life, but she didn't have a lot of experience outside the small town of Emmons. She didn't have a lot of experience with men, unless she counted two short relationships—one in high school and one in college. She was still all-too wary after the last one. He'd been too good-looking for his own good, and apparently for hers too. She'd decided she'd be fine on her own and didn't need a boyfriend or a husband.

Why had her mind strayed that far? She must be exhausted. She needed to find her dad's killer so she could somehow move forward.

The men sat watching her, obviously expecting an answer to their big question—protection detail or not?

"Finnley." Ayden's voice drew her attention from Caine. Had she been staring? Heat flooded her cheeks. Oh, no. Even worse. "If you feel uncomfortable working with Caine—"

"No, of course not. It's not that." Wasn't it?

Next to her, Too Good Looking for His Own Good shifted. He wore jeans and a polo shirt that stretched across his chest. His shoulders were broad, and his arms were ropy. Had she ever seen arms like that? Why had she looked at his arms or noticed them at all? *Oh, boy.*

"Then what is it?" he asked.

"I didn't mean it that way. It's fine."

Ayden stared at his desktop and tapped away on the keyboard. "I could rework Everly's schedule…"

"No." Finnley stood. "I… You're right. I probably need protection until we know what's going on." She looked between the brothers and tried to project confidence. "I'm good with Caine working protection detail while he investigates. I mean, how does this work exactly? I've never done anything like this. I've never had to?" She hung her head and then stood tall again. She had to see this through. "So what's next?"

Ayden turned his attention to his iPad now. "Just a few documents to sign, and then Caine will—" The cell on his desk buzzed, and he glanced at it. "Excuse me. I have to take this. Caine, you can finish up the details." He snatched up the cell, pushed the iPad torward Caine and left him alone with Finnley in his office.

Caine frowned as if he wasn't happy with Ayden's departure, but he dragged the iPad over to him and scrolled through pages. Finnley took the time to take in his features. His jaw was strong and angular, and his skin was tanned. He had wavy brown hair that hung to his collar and long dark lashes over hazel eyes. Again, she thought he was too good-looking for his own good—just like the jerk that broke her heart.

One of many things Dad had taught her was that she should never judge a book by its cover. She shouldn't hold it against Caine that he was handsome. She shoved those ridiculous unbidden thoughts away.

Finding Dad's murderer was her priority. But could she work with Caine without feeling awkward? She hoped so, because it wasn't like she had a lot of options.

"Finnley." His voice was gentle, and his hazel eyes held compassion. "Take a deep breath. It's going to be okay. You've been through a lot, and you need help. You came to the right place. Even though I'll be working with you personally, you have a whole team in your corner. So try to relax and trust me."

Trust you? I don't even know you!

Using the iPad, he showed her a document and where to sign with the Apple pen. He was methodical and patient as he explained how protection services worked, and she found herself relaxing with him, after all.

Caine set the iPad aside and looked at her. His expression softened. "So the sheriff didn't believe you. I'm sorry about that."

"And after I was run off the road, I overheard the deputy who found me telling Sheriff Henderson that I was being emotional and had just overreacted. That deer were thick this time of year. A stormy, rainy evening didn't help."

Do not cry. Do not cry. Finnley blinked back the tears. She wouldn't let this guy see how weak and shaky she really felt inside. "I don't care if they don't listen to me."

"I know. That's why you're here." He offered a tenuous smile. Trying to earn her trust? "You made the right decision and took the first big step. You're now officially a client."

Caine remained in the chair, acting relaxed, as if he had all the time in the world and was just waiting for her to fully grasp the circumstances and tell him she was ready.

"So what happens next?" she asked.

"I grab my gear, and we head home."

We? Home? "What are you talking about? What do you mean?" Finnley stiffened. She had no idea what she was getting into. Maybe this wasn't a good idea, after all. Her palms grew sweaty.

"It's okay," he said. "It's how protection works. At least, it's how we do it. Every situation is different. We want your life to be as normal as possible for as long as possible. I'll keep you safe. You don't have to feel nervous about me being around you or at your house. I'll make sure no one is there when we arrive and that you're safe while you are at home. Sound good?"

I'm not so sure. "I mean...you work 24/7?"

"During a protective detail, I can. Sometimes we trade out. We're constantly assessing the circumstances and shifting as necessary. I need to see your place. Protect and investigate. We'll make changes if we need to make them. That sounds reasonable, doesn't it?"

She was obviously showing him just how nervous she was because he kept trying to reassure her. "I guess. Sure." She could do this. She had to do this. It was going to be okay.

He stood and ushered her out of the office.

What am I doing? What am I doing?

What choice did she have? She couldn't let her father's murderer go. Justice had to be served.

She was going to have to learn to trust this stranger—Caine Honor—to both investigate her father's murder and protect her, even if him invading her space made her uncomfortable.

She would feel uncomfortable even if it were his sister, Everly, on protective detail, but Caine made her breath hitch every time she looked at him. This was going to be awkward. But that was all on her.

There was only one way to find out if this was going to work. As he led her out of the facilities and down to the garage, she took in the surroundings before her gaze landed once again on Caine.

He was a little taller than her and had a lithe physique. Kind of like a tennis player. He had the most intense eyes. He'd walked into the room, and his presence had slammed into her even through her grief and anger. She didn't understand her reaction to him. Even if he could protect her and help her find who killed her father, she still had a feeling, a very strong feeling, that he was dangerous in his own way.

But Finnley was up to the challenge.

Since Finnley's vehicle was "toast", as she put it, Caine drove from West Ridge, the suburb outside Tacoma where Honor Protection Specialists was located, toward Emmons. The small town was located much closer to Mount Rainier, the most prominent mountain in the region. The area was popular with tourists and photographers and loved by locals as well.

"How do you like living so close to the mountain?"

"Mountain? You mean active volcano." Her chuckle sounded nervous.

He suspected she was still uncomfortable with him, but he understood that. They would both feel awkward with each other for a while. Getting used to a stranger invading your personal space was always hard at first. He hoped that awkwardness would fade quickly, for her sake.

"I've never understood why they call the mountain active," he said.

"According to what I've read, it's *geologically* active. You and I can't see that. But scientists say that it has surface geothermal activity. Mount Rainier erupted one hundred fifty years ago and is expected to erupt again."

"Really." Caine should pay more attention. "Does that bother you?"

"Does it bother me that the government considers Mount Rainier a potentially dangerous volcano? Nah. Everyone has to die someday…" Her words faded at the end.

Caine wanted to kick himself. How had this conversation digressed to them talking of death on the heels of her father's murder, not to mention that her life was in danger as well.

Great. You're starting off so well on this trial run. He fumbled around for what to say next. *Don't worry, HPS will keep you from being murdered, at least.*

Best not to say anything and let Finnley direct the conversation or instead choose quiet. He steered along the road and enjoyed the silence. It was a clear day, and the mountain loomed ahead in the distance as they approached Emmons. It seemed to underscore their doom and gloom conversation.

"Emmons is named after the largest glacier on Mount Rainier," she finally said. "Dad hiked to the summit every year. But this year, he canceled the hike." She sniffled and looked out the passenger window. "We were planning to go on a cruise."

Caine had worked a lot of protection details, but none of them had involved a sensitive and vulnerable woman like Finnley. For some reason, she stirred up memories of Sophie in him.

That was not good.

Not professional.

He would give this a day or two and hope for the best, then he might need to tell Ayden he wasn't the best fit. Switching out clients didn't happen often, but it *did* happen. Sometimes there was a personality conflict. That wasn't the case here. It was more that Caine was feeling vulnerable and raw. He didn't want Ayden to know that, though.

The sniffles died down. Finnley had apparently gathered her composure and turned her face forward again. That was Caine's signal to focus on the investigation and not matters of the heart, which had absolutely no place here.

"When was he supposed to go hiking?" He hadn't read all the details in the case file Ayden had compiled, but that was okay. He preferred to hear it from her firsthand and then study the file for more answers later.

"He would have been up on the mountain hiking next week, but then he made plans for a cruise. He wanted to leave early to stay in a hotel in Seattle. I went to the drugstore to get a few supplies, and when I got back…"

She stared out the window again, and all he heard was sniffles.

Would she be able to get through all his questions without crying? He hoped so. The sound cut through his heart.

"Finding your father dead like that was terrible, Finnley. It's understandable that talking about it is upsetting. But you also understand that I need to ask questions, right?"

"Yes. I'm sorry."

Caine knew about terrible scenarios personally. He'd been through one years ago—and held a dying woman in his arms— the woman he'd loved. Sophie was the reason he'd sworn off love.

"No need to apologize. When you're ready, I want all the details that you can remember, but we have time since we'll be spending a lot of it together."

He couldn't be sure that was true, though, if he decided that he wasn't the best fit for her case. But what kind of jerk would he be to gain her trust and then leave. No. He wouldn't do that to her. Caine could be professional and not let his personal reservations get in the way.

It would be up to Finnley to decide if she couldn't work with him.

He had a feeling that she was stronger than she knew, but she was also more vulnerable than she realized. He had to put his memories and past aside to help Finnley find her way through her own tragedy.

She said nothing more, and they finally entered the Emmons city limits. Caine steered down Main Street of the small town.

"The shop—Wilbanks & Co.—is up a block and on the right," she said. "We live… Um, I live…in the apartment over the shop. You can park in front along Main Street or in the back. We don't have a designated parking spot even though we live in a downtown apartment, but it works."

"I'll park in the back." He preferred that the whole town didn't see she was home or that she had arrived in Caine's red Toyota 4Runner. "At least we're getting here before dark. I want to clear everything."

"Clear everything? In English please. I don't understand detective-speak, or protection-speak."

She would be learning more than she wanted to know by the time this was over. "Check to make sure that no one is waiting in your apartment." Or has set any kind of bomb or trap.

"Or that there are no monsters under the bed?"

"Yes." He chuckled. "That too."

"I'm not waiting in the car while you clear the apartment and shop." She shifted to unbuckle her seat belt.

"Fair enough. Just stick close. Do as I say. Understood?"

"Understood." She started to open the door.

"Wait," he said.

"For what?" Finnley looked at him, her brows arching.

"Just wait, okay? I'm waiting and watching. I like to see if there's anything out of the ordinary before jumping out of my vehicle. Is someone lurking in the shadows waiting for you to get home. That kind of thing."

"Now you're giving me the creeps."

"It's best to be cautious. So do you see anything out of the ordinary?"

She shook her head, and a soft smile emerged. He hadn't seen her smile until now, but what a weird time to smile. Was she even looking for anything strange? Would she know if something wasn't right? He rubbed his temple and stared out the window.

A few minutes went by. "I think we're good." *I hope.* "Time to move."

He'd backed into the far corner so he could watch the building, but there were woods behind them. He needed to clear those too at some point. Maybe the deputy was correct in his assessment that Finnley had overreacted and no one had tried to run her off the road, but Caine would give her the benefit of the doubt until he learned more.

Gun at his side and ready, he got out and grabbed his gear from the back. She'd already climbed out of his Toyota 4Runner and waited. He led her to the back of the building, and she unlocked the door.

"The apartment is upstairs. The shop is downstairs. Simple enough."

"Let me clear the apartment and you can get settled upstairs, then I'll make sure the store is fine. I know the sheriff did a cursory collection of evidence and dusted for prints, but I'll do my own evidence search and go from there."

Caine cleared the small three-bedroom apartment, living room and decent-sized kitchen. The place was decorated with bookshelves filled with dusty books that made his nose itch. After clearing the apartment, he headed downstairs.

"I'm going with you, Caine."

"Stick close."

She followed and gestured to the door to the shop. "It's not locked. Go ahead."

Ready to face anything, he entered the back of the shop.

Finnley leaned through the door, flipped on the lights, and then stood back and waited, but she didn't pass the threshold.

To let him make sure no one was here? Or because she didn't want to see the place where she'd found her father dead on the floor with a bullet to the head?

THREE

Finnley couldn't breathe. Images of finding her father accosted her as she stood in the doorway. Paralyzed her.

She had to be strong if she was going to make it through this ordeal, but Finnley couldn't make herself cross the threshold. She hadn't stepped back into the shop since she'd found Dad's body. Squeezing her eyes shut, she took a few calming breaths.

If nothing else, she didn't want Caine looking through the shop and Dad's things without her. The shop was a vintage stationery store and held hundreds, if not thousands of items, including stationery, cards, wax seals, inkwells, vintage papers, maps and posters.

Unshed tears welled in her eyes, and she forced herself to take a breath and blink back the tears.

I can do this.

Finnley took one step over the threshold and into the shop. Finally, she stepped through the door and drew in the musty smell that came from the building itself but also the vintage items. Her father had been old too—seventy-five. That was much older than most fathers of women her age. She was only twenty-seven.

Finnley admitted that she'd lived a protected life. Other than in books, she hadn't adventured much farther than the town of Emmons. Because of that, she felt timid and inadequate in Caine's very capable and obviously skilled presence. That was on her, not him. He hadn't said anything or behaved in a way that told her he thought she was naive or lacked street smarts.

What were street smarts in Emmons? The small town hadn't experienced any real crime—especially not since her dad's death had been ruled a suicide. Still, his death had shocked the community. She'd loved her life here. And now someone had shattered it for reasons unknown. Finnley wouldn't stop until she found out who killed her father and why.

She watched Caine's every move as he walked around the shop, appearing to take in every detail. While she watched, she continued to think through what had happened, mentally facing the horror of that day once again.

While she couldn't read his mind completely, she thought she might just be able to on one point.

"I know what you're thinking," she said.

"Oh?" He looked up at her, brows arched and eyes sharp as a hawk. "What's that?"

"You're wondering about this business." She moved to stand closer and see what he'd been looking at on the wall. Vintage calendars. He was probably bored out of his mind.

"What do you mean?" He continued, moving slowly and studying everything.

"Come on. It's a shop filled with papers for note taking and letter writing. Vintage stop. Maps. Pretty Victorian-era stuff. You're probably wondering what man would want a shop like this?"

"I wasn't. I'm simply interested to know more about your father, but not because of his choice in shopkeeping," Caine said. "Tell me about him."

Where did she even start? She drew in a calming breath and tried to forget that Dad was no longer alive.

"Well. Let's see… He was old-fashioned in every way. He loved his privacy and to spend time in old books." As she reminisced, her heart filled with warmth and love. So much love. "At the same time, he was the most giving person, but he remained in the background. Anonymous."

And I loved that about him. So did everyone else!

Caine turned to face her. His intense hazel eyes were overpowering. Did he know that? Was it just her that reacted this way to his scrutiny? His gaze softened and a warmth tickled her insides. He said nothing, and she knew he was waiting for her to tell him more about Dad. That made her heart smile. Caine was someone that cared. She relaxed, just a little, and thought she might be able to at least feel comfortable with him around all the time—at least, until this was over.

"Like I was saying, he helped people behind the scenes," she whispered because her throat grew thick with emotion. "Gave them money."

"Can you give me some specific examples?"

"He delivered a washing machine to a widow when hers broke down and couldn't be fixed. Everything he did to help others, he did anonymously. He refused to take credit." Those unshed tears once again filled her eyes, and she had to look at something over Caine's shoulder. "I could keep going."

"You've told me a lot already, Finnley. Catch your breath." He turned away from her and continued his slow perusal. She was grateful for the way he gave her space to process her grief.

The shop was so packed with stuff that a person could spend hours or days looking through it all. If there was some hidden clue that could lead them to Dad's killer, it could take a lifetime to discover.

"Sounds like everyone loved your father. Even though he supposedly liked to remain anonymous, I get the sense that most everyone in town knew he was kind and generous."

He sounds like Sheriff Henderson right now. A murder required motivation. "What you say is true. I realize there is no obvious motivation for murder, but that doesn't mean my father committed suicide."

Leaning against the wall, she tried to calm down. She was letting the sheriff get to her again. She gulped for air.

"You're right, Finnley. I agree, and we'll find out the truth. But you need to calm down and learn to breathe through your frustration."

She did as Caine instructed and drew in a deep breath. She couldn't help him if she sank deeper into sorrow or let everything overwhelm her. Finnley meandered toward the front of the door and stopped.

Night was falling, and she could see out into the street, and everyone could see inside the store.

"I could have sworn…"

"What's that?" he asked from the back of the store.

"Nothing." Maybe she'd been out of her mind with grief and only thought she'd pulled the shades on the windows and the door.

Her attention must have drawn Caine's to the windows. In a few strides, he was at the front of the store and pulled the shades down.

She hugged herself, hating the paranoid thoughts that came to her. Could someone have been watching them just now? She checked the door to make sure it was locked and saw that the Closed sign was hung in full display.

When she turned around, she saw Caine had gone into the office at the back of the shop. She went to follow him but hesitated moving all the way into the space.

Her throat constricted. This was where she'd found her father. Instead of looking at the office or the floor, she focused on Caine's back. He had his hands on his hips, so maybe that's what made his shoulders look even broader. His wavy hair was caught up in his jacket collar. She shouldn't be thinking about the way he looked, but it was hard not to.

That saying about judging a book by its cover was turning out to be so true when it came to Caine. Though she was still in the early pages of his story, he seemed to be kind and sensitive and compassionate, and not at all wrapped up in himself. But she would hold her judgment until the very end. She'd thought Anthony was all those things at first.

"So you worked here with your father. Just the two of you?" Caine's question pulled her attention back to the situation at hand.

The office closed in around her, and nausea swirled.

He reached for her, stopping short of touching her arms. "Are you okay?" His eyes were filled with deep concern.

She nodded but couldn't speak right away. "I'll be okay. To answer your question, yes. Now and then, Mr. Patel—he owns the electronics repair shop next door—would watch our shop too, but that was rare. That said, Dad had arranged for Mr. Patel to watch it while we were gone on the cruise."

Caine nodded and exited the office, lifting his gaze to the ceiling. "Too bad you didn't have security cameras."

Security cameras. "I… I wasn't thinking straight when I spoke to the sheriff, but Dad planned to have cameras installed."

"That's a good idea for anyone these days. But I need to know more. Like, did he mention this recently?"

Caine was watching her again, and she wished he wouldn't, even if that was an unreasonable request.

"Recently. Yes. Days ago, in fact. He was going to contact a security company to install them, but I don't know if he ever did. Now that I think about it, it must be related to what happened." She looked up at him and held his gaze. *Do you believe me?*

"Why do you say that?" He looked at her like she was being paranoid. It was like talking to the deputy all over again.

"He'd been acting strange. He wanted to install security cameras, and he hiked the summit with Greg every year, and this year, he planned a cruise? We were leaving early for it too.

Those behaviors are unusual for him." She pressed her hands against her head and fisted her hair. Angry tears burst out. "I should have known something was wrong. I'm so stupid."

"No, Finnley, no. You're not stupid. You couldn't have known."

The next thing she knew, he'd wrapped his arms around her, comforting her.

She felt like an idiot. She didn't want this from him. But his arms offered protection, his gentle voice soothed her, and his tenderness cut through her pain until she could finally breathe. She released a long, heavy sigh and stepped back.

After wiping her eyes, she looked him in the eyes, letting him know she was okay, that she was strong. His brows were furrowed and the depth of his concern for her sent her heart racing. This guy was intense.

"I'm okay now."

He nodded and started perusing the store again. Or was he simply trying to put distance between them?

"He'd been working later than normal," she said. "I'd hear a noise and come down and find him working in his office at weird hours. So like I said, he'd been acting strange. Only I didn't see it for what it was."

Caine crossed his arms as he stood in front of Dad's desk. "Could the store have been having financial issues?"

She shook her head. "I asked him about that, but Dad assured me there was nothing for me to worry about."

Caine lifted his face to hers. "And you didn't believe him."

"No. I *did* believe him."

And that's the problem. Because it was now all too obvious that her father had lied.

Caine's heart went out to Finnley. She looked much younger than she was and seemed too trusting, even when it came to trusting her father. But if someone murdered Frank Wilbanks, they must have had a reason. Even a supposedly random act of murder had motivation behind it.

Frank hadn't been in the wrong place at the wrong time. No one had burglarized the store and then killed him because he was a witness. At least not as far as Caine could tell. Nothing had been stolen.

The picture Finnley drew of her father couldn't possibly be colored with murder. Why would anyone want her father dead? Caine thought maybe her father kept secrets from Finnley. That was often the case in situations like this.

Finnley appeared so distressed, and his chest ached at hearing her pain and desperation to prove that her father would never kill himself. Caine wanted to prove her right if he could. Of course, if it turned out she was right, an entire new set of serious problems would be opened up.

Regardless, he would go at this one hundred percent. He sucked in a breath. Time to get busy. He'd like to speak to Greg Jones and get his perspective on Frank, but one thing at a time.

"With your permission," Caine said, "I'll have Everly review the financial data and accounting books." He couldn't fathom Frank would be involved in organized crime or drugs, but stranger things had happened.

She wiped at her eyes again. They were puffy and red. "Sure. Of course. Anything you need."

He nodded. "Enough of this tonight. You're tired and need to rest."

She also needed time away from his questions. He started to exit the office, hoping to lead her back to the apartment and get her away from the spot where her father had died a horrible death.

"Tomorrow's the funeral," she said. "Will you be attending?"

"Of course. I'm protecting you, remember? I brought a suit, so I'll blend in." At the stairwell, he stood aside and gestured for her to go first. "You don't go anywhere, and I mean anywhere, alone. Understand? I'm with you at all times."

She arched a brow. "Everywhere?"

"You know what I mean. I'd prefer you didn't go to the apartment or the shop at any time of day or night without me first clearing it." She probably thought he was going overboard. Through experience, he knew that it paid to take all precautions.

She said nothing as she started up the stairs. He checked the back door and made sure the dead bolt was in place before catching up to her in the apartment. "Not only do you need to rest but you need to eat."

"I'm not hungry." She plopped on the sofa.

"You need to keep up your strength for what comes next."

"What comes next…" It wasn't a question.

She was overloaded, and he needed to dial the tension down and give her some space and time to think and rest, but he wasn't a therapist. He was here to protect her while discovering who had shattered her life and why.

"Just so you know, I don't plan to stand guard outside the apartment door all night. I'll be right here in your space. I want to make sure you're good with that."

She blinked up at him from the sofa. "I'm good with that."

Okay. Next on his list… He stood in the kitchen of the open-space apartment. He needed to assess the space with her in it and find the best place for him to set up. He hoped this assignment didn't last long, but if it did, he and Brett could trade out with the protection detail, or even Everly, if she wasn't too busy. They'd make it work.

Caine opened the fridge to look inside.

"Just make yourself at home." Her tone sounded sarcastic.

"You need to eat. What would you like?" The fridge was stocked. Either she or her father liked to cook and put the large kitchen to good use.

"I told you I'm not hungry."

"All right. If you don't want to tell me what you would like to eat, then be prepared for Caine's special."

"Caine's special?"

He pulled out onions, olives and tomatoes. Then he found angel-hair pasta in the cabinet. "Yeah. I make food with whatever I find."

"If you cook, that means I'll have to clean," she said. "I don't feel like cleaning. Why don't we just do takeout?"

That could give someone an opportunity to get close to her. "I can cook *and* clean."

"How do you protect me if you're making dinner? Can you really investigate, protect, cook and clean all at the same time?"

Working with her and being in her space could reveal nuances and perhaps lead to the reason her father was murdered. "Nobody is getting through me to get to you no matter what I'm doing." He sent her a grin, but it fell flat even to him.

He'd failed before. He would never fail again.

But Finnley wasn't Sophie. This situation wasn't that. So he wasn't sure why those memories kept rushing through him.

After dinner, Finnley yawned and headed to her bedroom. He would take up residence on the sofa and keep a lookout through the windows, as well as occasionally head downstairs to check on the store. He'd only get a few hours of sleep tonight, but he knew how to sleep with one eye open from his days in the army.

He turned the lights off in the living room. Some protectors preferred the lights on, but he liked the advantage he had right now. There was just enough light for him to see, but not enough to make him a target. He'd tasked Everly with looking into the store's books and Frank personally and had also arranged for security cameras to be installed. Caine couldn't find evidence that Frank had contacted a security firm to install any. Maybe he'd been shot and killed before he'd had the chance to.

Caine went over everything he knew in his head. Frank had planned a cruise instead of his usual hike to the summit. He'd insisted on leaving days before the cruise was scheduled. He'd also planned to install security cameras—for safety while they were here or to monitor while they were gone? Then he was found with a bullet to the head. Self-inflicted or murder?

Someone had also tried to run Finnley off the road.

That made it more obvious to him. Caine wasn't sure what the sheriff's department's problem was, but he would have to play nice and work with them to bring them over to his side. The more people working on this, the safer Finnley would be, and the faster the case would be resolved. Emmons didn't have a police department and relied solely on the county sheriff and her deputies. They covered a large county and rarely had crime issues.

Looked like things were changing.

The investigation in process, at least via Honor Protection Specialists, Caine would focus his attention on watching the place for tonight.

If someone came at Finnley here, he'd need to move her. He didn't know yet if anyone would be that bold, and he needed time here so he could potentially discover what had happened the night Frank died. Had one of his acts of kindness earned him a death sentence?

A scream erupted from the bedroom. Caine raced across the apartment with his gun drawn. Finnley stood back from the window and gasped for breath.

"Someone's out there." She pointed at her window. "Someone… Someone was outside."

He moved to the window and peered between the curtain and the wall and saw no one. But they could have rushed into the shadows of the woods.

"What are you doing?" she snapped. "Go after them?"

"I'm not leaving you here alone. What did you see?"

"Someone was looking into your 4Runner, peering through the window. He looked up at the second floor as if he was looking right at me. As if he caught me watching him." Her voice shook.

Anger coursed through him. He really wanted to find the jerk out there, but protection was his priority. "Did you get a good look at him?"

"It was too dark."

Had she really seen someone? "Why were you looking out the window?"

"What does it matter? Don't you believe me? Are you like everyone else who thinks I'm imagining things?"

Now she really was overreacting, but he understood her frustration.

He set his gun aside and approached her to gently press his hands against her arms. "Finnley…" His voice came out husky for some strange reason. He hadn't meant that tone. "Of course, I believe you. But I'm not going to leave you here and go chasing someone into those woods. I'm here to protect you. Your life is more important than anything."

He caught a flash of tears on her cheeks. Hadn't she cried enough? Been through enough? He ached, watching her suffer like this. Though he wanted to draw her into his arms like he'd done before, he couldn't make a habit of it.

Comfort wasn't a service Honor Protection Specialists offered—at least not officially. "It's going to be okay. Nobody is getting through me."

For what must have been a few brief seconds, he fought that need to hold her.

She rubbed her arms and released a heavy sigh. "I'm sorry I freaked out."

"It's understandable. Get some rest if you can. Try to sleep.

I'll check the shop downstairs and then I'll be right back." He wished he'd flatly refused this assignment. He was entirely too vulnerable at the moment. His siblings had all found their significant others and memories of the beautiful dark-eyed Italian he'd fallen for were bombarding him now. She'd counted on him, and he'd failed her. He couldn't let himself love like that again. Caine didn't think he could take the pain of losing someone else he loved.

Finnley was such a tender soul, and she touched his heart. No matter his personal struggles, he'd see this through and protect her.

She nodded, and he closed the door behind him, moving downstairs to check the locks again. He peeked through a window at the back, noting the bars over them, and saw nothing. Then he watched out the front of the shop, lifting the shade enough to see. The town was quiet and security lights dimly lit Main Street. A cat tiptoed down the sidewalk.

Then a stealthy, shadowed form peered out from an alley across the street before quickly ducking back into a dark alley. Caine palmed his gun in his holster and gritted his teeth. He wanted to go after the figure in the shadows, but he'd told Finnley he wasn't chasing anyone into the woods. Her safety was his priority.

FOUR

The next day, Caine steered the 4Runner out from behind the buildings where he'd left the vehicle in the public parking last night.

Dead brown leaves blew and swirled along the eerily empty Main Street. The cold fall day seemed appropriate for the funeral of a local pillar of the community.

Some shops along the street were closed. In memory of and out of respect for Frank Wilbanks? Were the proprietors attending the funeral?

Driving Finnley to the graveside service, Caine felt completely out of place. He was hired protection. Did the townspeople know that she'd hired him? Any threat to her certainly knew his vehicle by now. How did she want him to introduce himself?

He should ask.

But she was solemn and in a pensive state of mind. Who could blame her? He hesitated breaking the silence and instead simply followed the directions per the map on the dash.

"No," Finnley said. "You need to turn right. Take the next right."

"What?"

"She's not giving you the right directions. In fact, just follow that car ahead of you. That's Sheriff Henderson. She'll be at the funeral."

He turned right. "Do you want people to know who I am and what I do?"

"I'd prefer to keep that between us, if that's okay? Is there a protocol on that? What's the best way to go?"

"No specific protocol. Each situation is different. I think keeping our partnership private is a good idea for now, but who would you like me to pretend to be in case anyone is looking or asks?"

Finnley remained quiet. He glanced her way. Her hair hung forward, and even on this cloudy day, she wore sunglasses to hide her pain and keep it private.

"Finnley?"

"I'm thinking. I've lived here my whole life. I went to school here and attended the local small college. Dad had no other family. I have no idea. Who can you be?"

That was a question he'd never been asked before. "Does anyone else know anything about your extended family? Or your father's friends he made before coming to Emmons?" Everly was even now trying to learn more about Frank Wilbanks and who he was, where he'd come from before landing in Emmons. "I could be the grandson of an old friend of your father's. He wanted to come to the funeral but was too sick, so I came in his stead to give my condolences."

"That could work. We'll need a name. What's your name?"

"I'll stick with Caine. Makes it easier. You don't happen to know any of your father's old friends, do you?"

"Other than Greg, not really. I don't know if he'll be here or not. I don't even know if he realizes Dad is gone. I…" Her voice cracked with the words, the sentence she couldn't finish.

"It's okay. Don't worry. The less talking we do at the funeral, the better. Talk to *me*, though, if you need to. I'll stick by your side, but I might stand back a bit to observe."

"Observe?"

"Get a feel for everyone there. I don't want to scare you,

but it's not out of the question to think that his killer could be there."

A small gasp escaped her. He wished he could pull the words back.

"Please, don't think about it," he said. "Nothing is going to happen at the funeral. You'll be fine. I shouldn't have said that."

"You need to be up-front with me. Don't keep *anything* from me. Do you understand?"

"Absolutely." He would tell her everything he believed she needed to know. Caine followed the sheriff's vehicle through a gate and down a rutted path to park on the grass next to about thirty cars.

The wind gusted, and the trees swayed. If it started to rain, it would turn into a cliché. He ran around to open the door for her, and surprisingly, she let him.

She slipped out of the seat and adjusted her sunglasses.

He stood in her path, blocking her way. "I'm here if you need me, Finnley. If you're ready to leave, just say the word. I'll get you out of here."

Caine moved aside, and she merely nodded, her eyes shielded behind the glasses. He wished he could see her big brown almond-shaped eyes, but then again, seeing her raw grief could tear him apart. He needed to be less emotionally connected to her, but he feared it was already too late.

Caine walked next to Finnley as she slowly made her way toward the people waiting for the graveside service to begin. The group spoke in normal tones until Finnley approached, then their voices turned to whispers and murmurs and sympathetic or pitying looks. Finnley could be too wrapped up in her grief to notice. Would she engage in conversation? He'd been to a few funerals, and to houses of those left behind, but every family, every region mourned differently. He wasn't sure what to expect here.

Finnley approached a man in a dark suit whom Caine assumed would officiate the service. When the man spoke, Caine immediately knew he was the officiator, the pastor of a local church perhaps, or simply the funeral home pastor.

Caine used that opportunity to step away from Finnley and move closer to a tree that stood back from the canopy erected to protect the grave from the weather in case it rained. He wanted to watch those in attendance and discreetly took pictures of the crowd. Finnley took a seat, and others gathered and sat next to her, preventing Caine from sitting, but he wasn't family. He wasn't a friend. He had no place next to her. No one spoke to him or approached to ask his relation to Finnley, which was fine with him. It gave him more opportunity to observe the crowd.

Like he'd told Finnley, the killer could be in attendance. Maybe he could get a list of the attendees who signed the book up front and compare with those in town who did *not* attend.

The pastor spoke highly of Frank, and others stood to share tearful testimonies of what the man had done. Delivered groceries. Paid a medical bill. Secured transportation. All behind the scenes.

But they'd all known who had been behind the good deeds.

The man wanted no credit. No praise.

Oddly, the words moved him, shifting something deep inside. Frank Wilbanks was a model of humanity and a pillar of the community. Caine hoped he could be as well thought of. The man hadn't deserved his untimely death, and all Caine could do was find justice for Frank and make sure his daughter stayed alive.

Finnley sat in the chair and tried to hold back the tears, but it was no use. They continued to stream down her face. She was so glad she'd thought to wear the sunglasses even on such a gloomy, gray day. It was so fitting for her father's funeral.

She was mostly left to herself and in her own grief. Still, listening to people from town sharing the good deeds her father had done, hearing their admiration and grief, warmed her heart and broke it at the same time. It was all she could do to sit there and not get up and scream in anger that someone had murdered him.

Fortunately, she heard no murmured, whispered talk at all about the alleged suicide, but she suspected that in their own homes, they all whispered he'd killed himself. Perhaps they were also whispering that she was unwilling to accept the truth of that.

And they were right.

Dad didn't kill himself.

She'd cried herself dry, and no more tears appeared, at least not the kind that could stream down her cheeks. The pain was there, nonetheless, and her body shuddered. Her shoulders shook.

Everyone was watching.

Finally, Pastor Graley finished, and the official services were over. Various neighbors and friends from town finally decided to approach to give their condolences, but Finnley's throat was tight with emotion, and she could barely speak a word. People were watching her. She could feel their stares. She sensed someone watching her…in a different way.

That was ridiculous. Everyone was here to support her and to grieve with her.

Finally, everyone left, and Finnley was there alone except for the pastor.

She stood and moved toward the casket. Now that everyone else had left, the casket would be lowered. Caine had remained at the tree where he'd been for the entire service. In her peripheral vision, she caught him suddenly moving.

A chill crawled over her, and she turned to look behind her. A sudden gust of wind inflated the canopy tent and whipped it up into the air so violently the stakes pulled right out of the ground. The wind carried the crumpled mass of material toward the woods. Finnley's heart jumped to her throat as she tried to steer clear.

Where was Caine? He'd been right there, and now he was gone. There was a flash of color in the woods behind the tent that flapped against the trees where it had been caught.

"Caine!" she shouted and rushed to the edge of the woods. "Caine!"

Why had he gone deeper into the woods? All she could think was that he was chasing after whoever she'd sensed watching her. He wouldn't want her running into the woods alone and distracting him. She was surprised that he'd left her side, though.

God, please protect Caine.

She should get to the 4Runner and get inside. Lock the doors. That was the best way for her to help him. Get somewhere safe in case of the worst-case scenario. She wasn't sure if this was it, but not being able to find her bodyguard seemed likely to fall within that category. She turned around and hurried across the cemetery toward the 4Runner.

Pastor Graley called after her. "Finnley. Are you all right?"

She turned and continued walking backward toward the vehicle. "I'm sorry. I have to go. I'll contact you later. Thank you!" She rushed to the vehicle and then remembered it belonged to Caine. She couldn't get inside without the fob. She felt so stupid, but she couldn't think straight.

That same chill crawled over her as if she was being watched. Or was she finally letting everything get to her and really being paranoid? She rubbed her arms as she shuddered. Someone was near her.

Listening, she stood stock-still, but the wind had whipped up, and the trees were rustling. Perfect for anyone to creep up behind her.

Someone was right behind her. She knew it!

Before she could whirl around to look, someone gripped her arms and yanked her toward a dense copse near the parked vehicles, pulling her deeper into the woods. Finnley tried to scream, but a hand covered her mouth as her attacker pulled a black bag over her face. She kicked and fought, panic rising in her chest.

I'm going to die now! Just like my father!

God, help me!

Her attacker lifted her as she kicked out her legs in a wild frenzy, and she suddenly found traction against a tree trunk. Finnley pushed against the tree and flipped out of the man's grip. She turned and fought, even though she couldn't see a thing. He tried to grip her arms once again, but she slammed the heel of her palm forward and felt it connect. She heard the sickening crack of his nose. *Yes!*

She yanked the bag off her head and kicked him in the groin. He bent over in pain, dropping a knife.

A knife?

Finnley turned and ran. She hadn't gotten a good look at his face—what with his nose smashed up and him bent over in pain—but she wouldn't wait around to give him another chance to take her and kill her.

She raced out of the woods and was almost back to the cemetery when she tripped and fell face-first into a soft patch of grass.

A hand touched her, and she flipped over and screamed and kicked. Only it was Pastor Graley.

Caine appeared, gasping for breath. "Finnley, what happened?"

Her throat constricted, and she could barely get out the words, but she pointed. "Someone grabbed me. Tried to drag me away."

Pastor Graley and Caine looked at the woods. His features grim, Caine assisted her onto her feet. She dusted off her black slacks.

"Aren't you going to go after him?" She glanced at Caine.

"I didn't see anyone," Pastor Graley said.

Great. This just got better and better.

"You keep an eye on her. I'm going to see if I can find her attacker," Caine said and took off into the woods.

"Be careful, Caine! He had a knife!" she called after him.

Pastor Graley led her over to his vehicle. "You can sit inside while we wait."

"No, thank you." She let her gaze search the woods for Caine, hoping he'd return soon unharmed. Hoping he'd find whoever had attacked her. "I should call the sheriff." Finnley fished her cell from her pocket and called Dispatch to report the attack. She was told a deputy would come to the cemetery as soon as he could get there.

Finnley heard the unspoken question in the dispatcher's voice. The sheriff had just been at the funeral. Who would attack her there?

"Finnley? Are you going to be all right?" Pastor Graley glanced into the woods. "I mean, how well do you know Caine?"

"Well enough that I trust him. I'll be fine."

The look on the pastor's face told her he wasn't convinced, but all he said was, "If you need anything, anything at all, you just call me. I'm not half a mile away from you. Mabel suggested you come and stay with us for a while if you want. I'm sure she must have mentioned that to you today."

Maybe. Lots of people had spoken to her, but Finnley couldn't remember most of it. "I'll be fine, and I promise I'll call if I need you." He deserved more than a nod from her.

"For anything. Even to talk. Do you need a ride back?"

"No. Caine can take me when he gets back."

Just then, her protection detail emerged from the woods,

half jogging and half walking, but not out of breath. Tension lines creased his face as he approached them.

"Did you find him?" Finnley asked.

"No. But I saw signs of a struggle in the woods."

"I called the sheriff's office, and they're sending someone out," she said.

"Good," he said. "It's not safe to wait around for too long."

Finnley glanced at Pastor Graley. "Thank you for waiting with me. I… I just want to look at the casket now that Caine is here. I want to be alone. It's okay, Pastor Graley. You don't have to stay."

He nodded, gave her a look of sympathy and squeezed her hands gently, then he hurried toward his car, the wind buffeting his tall, slim body. Trees swayed, and the canopy ballooned and rippled in the woods. She figured it might rip completely if someone didn't come and put it away. She had no idea who was in charge of such things.

"Caine, I need one last look. Please?"

"Finnley, someone just attacked you."

"And where were you? Where did you go? I came back to your car to get in and then realized I had no way to unlock it."

"I'm sorry about that. I thought you were safe here with the pastor and those men preparing to lower the casket and bury it. I saw someone in the woods, and I went to investigate. This is all on me. I'll never leave you again unless I'm sure you're protected."

"It's okay. I know it's not safe, but my father…"

"Okay. Sure. Let's go to the casket."

Two men stood to the side of the hole they had dug as she approached. Caine was right behind her.

They were waiting for her to leave so they could lower the casket. Finnley moved to stand next to it and pressed her hand across the smooth varnished white surface.

She had this one last moment to say goodbye to her father.

Dad...

Caine suddenly drew up next to her, saying softly, "We need to leave."

"But—"

"Now."

He ushered her toward his 4Runner.

"I was saying goodbye. I need to—"

"You hired me to protect you, and that's what I'm doing."

"What about the deputy?"

"I'll call and let them know we're leaving. They can look in the woods and ask you questions at the apartment."

At the vehicle, he practically shoved her inside. He climbed in the driver's side, started the engine and peeled away from the grave site, speeding down the rutted path.

"The whole funeral, I thought I felt someone watching. It was weird. I thought I was being paranoid. That I was over-reacting."

"Well, obviously, you weren't overreacting. Did you get a look at the man who grabbed you?"

"It happened so fast. He dragged me into the woods and put a bag over my head. I fought. Got him in the nose, and after I pulled the bag off my head, I got him in the groin and ran, but then I fell. I...didn't get a good look. He'd covered his face because his nose was bleeding. He was strong, and he had on a black jacket and beanie. What about you? You saw someone in the woods. Did you get a look?"

"No. I took a picture, so we'll see if I caught anything that can help us. But I shouldn't have left you. Please forgive me for that." He reached across the console and squeezed her hand.

"There's nothing to forgive." She savored the feel of his hand on hers and the reassurance that his grip and his words gave her. At the worst possible moment, a rush of warmth flooded her heart. The feelings that stirred inside were completely inappropriate given the circumstances. But even so, they rose up.

She freed her hand from his. She couldn't afford to let herself get attached to him or anyone, not after her two disastrous relationships. First in high school, she'd been young and stupid. She wouldn't blame herself for trusting a good-looking football guy who tried to take advantage of her. But she should have known better at the local college. She wasn't the kind of girl that good-looking guys—men like Caine—were attracted to.

Maybe Ezra was into her at the beginning, but it was hard to know. Hard to trust. In the end, he'd been seeing multiple women behind her back. She hadn't been enough for him. She was never enough.

Caine was sweet and tender and caring, and he seemed so much more than his *GQ* cover appearance, but she wouldn't be fooled a third time.

She watched the trees rush by along the road as he took them back to the shop and her apartment. He drove in silence, which was fine with her. The day had drained her completely.

"I'm still hoping the local law enforcement will join in the search for answers," he finally said. "Be prepared to answer questions when the deputy shows up."

"He won't listen."

"At some point, the sheriff's department will have to listen."

"That point might be too late." *Like if I'm dead.*

"You hired protection, Finnley, remember? Stick close to me, but you should know that we might need to move to a secure location."

"I'm not ready." Not yet.

FIVE

The next day, the security cameras arrived. While Finnley took a nap, Caine unpacked the box and read through the instructions. He'd had Everly order a top-of-the-line system, which typically would be installed by an expert. Caine didn't consider himself an expert, but he could install the cameras and figure out the app himself; that way he would be the only one who knew about his setup and the passcodes. It wasn't unheard of to learn a security system guy had been involved in a criminal scheme. Caine didn't trust this job to anyone else.

He put cameras at every corner on the outside, front and back, and inside the entryways, so every space could be seen from his phone or computer. Alarms would go off too if anyone should lurk around too close to Wilbanks & Co. at night.

The day was nice, not too hot and not too cold, but he was still sweating by the time he finished. He dropped the tools he'd found in a closet into the tool chest when his cell phone buzzed.

Everly.

He snatched it up and kept his voice down. "Got 'em installed."

"Good. Now, did you get them set up on your phone?"

"I will once I end the call."

Everly paused and then asked, "How is she?"

"She's sleeping now. That's why I'm keeping my voice down.

Yesterday was hard on her." The deputy had arrived two hours after the funeral and taken her statement. He'd gone by the woods but claimed he hadn't seen evidence of a scuffle in the woods. Caine assured Finnley that they were building a file, and this would all work in their favor.

Caine had already sent Everly the image he'd taken in the woods. But if he was chasing after someone in the woods, then who had grabbed Finnley?

"I can only imagine," she said.

"Thanks for asking." He wiped his hands with a towel.

"Anything else going on?"

"I'm not sure yet." He'd put the tools back later since he didn't want to wake Finnley. They were clanky.

"What's that supposed to mean?" she asked.

"Someone's definitely been lurking nearby. Watching. Good guy or bad guy, I don't know."

"Come on, Caine. Why would it be a good guy?"

He lifted a shoulder, though she couldn't see his reaction. "Could be someone else watching out for her."

"Is that what you really think?" Everly's tone was incredulous.

"I don't have enough facts."

"Sometimes you have to listen to your gut."

"My gut isn't sure." Now he was just messing with her head. Sort of.

Everly chuckled. "Anything else I can do to help?"

"Maybe. Her father owned a vintage shop. Art advertising posters. Victorian-looking stuff that I don't even know what to call. It's hard to imagine he could stay in business in such a small town without some kind of online presence. I couldn't find a website."

"Which is how most vintage stationery shops survive. It's definitely a niche market. That's a great observation. It could mean something, or it could mean nothing. Anything else?"

"Not yet. But I find it interesting that he became Finnley's father at forty-eight. She's twenty-seven, and he was seventy-five when he died."

"Are you just hashing through the facts with me? 'Cause you're not telling me anything I don't already know."

"I was thinking that he was in his seventies and supposedly hiked to the Mount Rainier summit every year?"

"Maybe that's why he opted for the cruise this year? I don't think you're ever too old to do things you love. Sounds like he was in really good shape."

"But how could he be in shape when, according to Finnley, he hung out in the store all the time?"

"Did she actually say that? Maybe he went to the gym?"

"You got me. I didn't ask her. Bottom line is I'd like you to dig around into his background."

"I'm already doing that."

"I'm not talking about a general search, birth certificate and all that. Dig deeper into his background. As I already mentioned, the store doesn't even have a website, and there's no social media either. The more I learn, the more it feels like something is off. And I *am* listening to my gut."

He blew out a heavy breath and rubbed his temples with one hand. "On the other hand, the guy draws pictures and binds books by hand. He's into nostalgia. Maybe he was just a Luddite, and I've got this all wrong."

Caine had moved into Frank's office and eased into the chair at his desk. Something he wouldn't have done if Finnley were here because she was sensitive about her father's things, and rightly so.

"Or maybe he thought it was nice to get away from electronics for a change," she said.

"I need to go if I'm going to get this app uploaded and the cameras hooked up. I need to check on Finnley too."

"Okay. Keep me updated."

"Will do."

Caine leaned forward, pressing his elbows on his thighs. He wanted to believe Finnley's father hadn't killed himself, but the converse of that meant more danger for Finnley. Finding the motivation for Frank's murder was key. When he stood, the chair caught on a floor mat, and that's when he spotted what looked suspiciously like a computer cable.

What? No...

Caine carefully moved the desk away from the wall. He followed the cable behind a bookshelf. Even though Finnley had given him permission to search the shop for evidence, he had a feeling that she wasn't going to like just how invasive he was about to get. To move the shelf, he needed to take the books off. Who was he kidding? She was going to freak out over this hidden computer cable. Maybe he could do it quickly and then get the books back in place. In the end, it didn't matter. He had to do this. He'd found something hidden and conspicuously out of place.

Caine took a picture of the shelf and the office so he could put everything back exactly where he'd found it. He stacked the books over next to the far wall and then started moving the shelf.

"What do you think you're doing?" Finnley stood in the doorway, a look of horror on her face.

She struggled to breathe. Caine had sucked the air from her lungs. She might collapse to her knees.

Dragging in a big breath, she found the words. "What. Are. You. Doing?" Hands out, trying to take in the scene, she rushed to the stack of books he'd removed. Dad's books. His personal collection. The books she believed he valued more than her at times. He'd been so protective of them. Didn't want anyone touching them.

And she'd never.

Would never.

She glared at Caine. "Get out. Get out of here!"

"Finnley, wait. I… I apologize. I should have asked you first, but listen—"

Finnley pointed at the door. "Get out of here."

She hoped he would leave so he wouldn't see her break down and sob. Her lip quivered. Oh, brother. She hated herself right now. She was making Dad's books more important than Caine. Than anything. Just like her father.

She dropped her arm and let her shoulders droop. The grief would take her down if she let it.

Caine held out his hand as if offering it to her. Or in surrender. She wasn't sure. "Finnley, please, just calm down and let me explain. I think your father hid something behind this bookshelf."

She was afraid to speak and just stared at him. *Go ahead. Try to talk your way out of this atrocity.* Something inside her feared what he would say. He was right to search. She'd hired him to investigate. But deep inside she'd hoped and prayed he wouldn't find anything that would point any fingers at her father. That someone killed him, but not because he had secrets.

Nausea roiled in her stomach. "I'm listening."

"I found wiring behind the desk that connects to something behind the bookshelf. It looks suspiciously like a cable of some kind. Like a computer cable. I could be wrong, but…"

What? He had to be wrong. Her father was so anti-technology. He carried a flip phone, and that was only because she insisted.

She took a slow step forward. Then another until she stood next to Caine. He showed her the cable.

This couldn't be right. This couldn't belong to her father. Shock might bowl her over. Curiosity overcame the sudden rush of blood to her head that was making her dizzy.

"Move the shelf. Let's see what's behind it." She had to get to the bottom of this.

Caine slid the bookshelf away from the wall and found a door. *A door?* Finnley stared, trying to comprehend this new development. *What is going on?*

He looked at her. *Waiting for permission?*

"Well, go on, open it. We've come this far." Thanks to Caine, who had been here all of forty-eight hours, whereas Finnley had lived here for twenty-seven years.

He opened the door, reached around for a light switch and then flipped it on, revealing a room with computers and monitors.

"There must be another way in," Caine said as if the site hadn't left him in shock. "I can't imagine him moving the books every time."

Heart pounding, Finnley viewed the contents of the office.

"Maybe he didn't move them every time because this doesn't belong to him. Maybe…maybe he didn't know about this." Right. She wasn't making sense. He'd owned the shop for years. This was all newer stuff. At least it looked rather modern and not something from the late eighties.

Dad knew all right.

Her knees shook at the thought. *He knew…*

Caine turned and gently gripped her upper arms while he looked into her eyes. His gaze was so intense she couldn't help but look at him, connect with him. He slowly nodded. "Take a deep breath, Finnley. I'm here with you. It's going to be okay."

She sucked in the stale air of the office and tried her best to compose herself.

"How is it going to be okay?" She stepped back and away from Caine, putting a little space between them and pushing back the shock. Or rather, swallowing it.

She swallowed this new, outrageous truth that was being crammed down her throat with the death of her father.

"This is clearly my father's office. An office he kept hidden from me. He lied to me. He kept this a secret from me. For years. My entire life! I… I didn't know my father at all."

She fought the need to run and flee. Losing that battle, Finnley turned and ran out of the secret office, through the other office and then into the store. Unlocking the front door, she flung it wide-open and rushed outside onto the sidewalk to get some fresh air.

The cold night air was nippy, and the light mist didn't help. But she had to put the shop and home she had shared with him behind her. Cars were parked along Main Street as patrons visited the shops that remained open. A few people walked the sidewalks, and what passed for rush hour traffic in Emmons was nearing an end.

Dad was gone and dead, and the world hadn't stopped because of it.

Her father—the only person she trusted. The only family she had in her life—she hadn't even truly known him. He'd kept some major secrets from her.

At the street corner, she pressed her hands against her midsection and leaned over, ready to lose it all here and now in front of anyone who cared to look. But really, no one cared. Dad's funeral had been yesterday, and today everyone moved on. Everyone except her.

"Finnley…" Caine tempered his voice, keeping it low, but she heard the desperation.

Caine hadn't moved on.

"This isn't safe. Please come back inside with me. I promise we'll figure this out. Don't you see? What we found could be the connection. This could give us the answers we need to know why your father was murdered."

She lifted her gaze to look at Caine. Too-good-looking-for-his-own-good Caine. Compassion filled his eyes. Compassion and determination. He held his hand out—an invitation to go with him.

Finish this.

"Come on." He shot her a tenuous grin. "Don't make my job to protect you any harder than it has to be. This isn't safe. Nor do I like leaving your shop open."

Finnley nodded. She took his hand, and they walked back to the Wilbanks & Co. shop together.

Once inside again, Caine cleared the upstairs and downstairs to make sure no monsters had entered after their brief departure.

Again.

This was her life for the foreseeable future. And thinking of foreseeable…

"I should have suspected this. I should have known he was hiding something. I feel so naive. Too trusting. How do I even know I can trust you, Caine?"

Finnley whirled to stare at him, search his eyes. She wanted to trust him, but in the end, she was only paying him to be here. She could only trust him so far.

"Finnley…your father loved you and cared for you very much. Whatever it was he hid from you was simply a matter of protecting you. I'm sure of it. Your trust in him was not misplaced."

She'd have to think on that for a while before she could fully accept it. "You haven't answered my question. What about you? How do I know I can trust you?"

"You don't." His pain-filled gaze confirmed his words. "At least, not yet. I'll just have to show you. Prove to you that you can trust me."

SIX

Caine had told Finnley he'd prove to her that he was trustworthy, but he also needed to prove to himself that her trust in him wasn't misplaced.

Not that he would ever willingly hurt Finnley by lying to her or failing her. The thought of it sent a pang through him. But even when he didn't mean to hurt someone, the hurt could come all the same when he failed to protect them. Images of Sophie rushed back to him. She'd trusted Caine…

He shook it off.

Thinking about Sophie now would mess him up royally. He couldn't afford to let his doubts cloud his thoughts or judgment.

"Are you ready, Finnley? Ready to finish what we started?"

"You mean in Dad's office?"

"Yes."

"I'm ready. I'm sorry that I ran off. I just needed air. I wasn't prepared to come downstairs to—"

"Your reaction was normal." He led her into the office and then the hidden office. "There has to be another entrance. I don't see him moving that shelf."

"Unless he just didn't need to get into this room often. Or ever."

Finnley was still trying to reconcile this discovery with the man she knew. Caine felt around the edges of the wall and part of it popped open to reveal a crawl space. Okay, so the man who climbed mountains also crawled through small spaces.

"I'm going through to see where this leads." Caine tugged his gun free.

"You're crawling through there with your gun?"

"Yes. I have no idea where it ends up."

"You said you were never leaving me again, so I'm going with you."

She had him there. Caine got down and crawled through the space until he came to a dead end. He pushed on the wall and discovered he was once again behind a fake shelf. He made it through and then stepped out into a hallway at the back entrance.

Finnley crawled out and stood, taking in the location of the other "secret" entrance.

"Well, whatever he used that space for, there was no easy way in and out." And with the words, Caine suspected she felt a measure of satisfaction.

This didn't seem to be a space that he visited often. Caine moved back into the office with the computer equipment. He took pictures and studied it, thinking what this could mean.

So far, Sheriff Henderson hadn't taken a lot of interest in Caine's reports. He'd reported the attack on Finnley at the funeral. He'd reported that he'd chased someone into the woods and that someone had been lurking near the shop. He understood that she had her hands full protecting a large geographic area. Fine with him.

He preferred to let Everly take charge of the forensic work. She could do it or use her connections.

"Do you happen to know who the company is in Wilbanks & Co."

"Me. Or at least, I always assumed it meant Dad and me." Finnley sat in the seat and stared at the computer. She reached forward.

"Don't…touch it," he said.

Her eyes narrowed. "I want to know what he was doing."

"As do I. I texted Everly, and she is arranging for the computers to be retrieved for forensic work. Everything will be documented for evidence purposes. It's best if you don't have anything to do with this."

Because who knows. Frank was murdered, and he could have been involved in criminal activity. Sophie's father's proximity to the Sicilian Mafia had put Sophie in danger. And now Finnley was in danger.

God, help me protect her…

And help me not to fall for her while I'm at it.

After what Caine had been through with Sophie, he hadn't believed that he had a heart left, but right now, his heart was breaking for this woman.

Her face visibly paled. He could see that she was running through those same scenarios. Time to take her in a different direction.

"What can you tell me about your mother?" he asked.

"Questions? Now?"

"Yes. There's a lot I still don't know. It'll take time to put the pieces together. This could be a big piece, or it might not be connected at all." Though he believed in his gut this hidden office and the computers held the key to Frank's murder. "Or we have a big piece here, and I need to find all the other pieces to see the whole picture."

"What could my mother have to do with anything? She's been dead for over two decades. I never knew her." Finnley stared at the wall and shook her head.

He could tell by the look in her eyes that her mind was far from this office. "Nothing makes any sense right now. I never knew my mother. Dad told me Agatha—that was her name— died in a fire. But…was that even true? I just don't know. Everything—all the photos we had—were lost. Dad said he had taken me to the park that day. He only had an old Polaroid shot of her taken years *before* I was born."

Her eyes found his then. "She was in her early thirties. Ten years younger than Dad when they met."

Finnley's eyes glazed over as she got up and walked out of the office.

His cell pinged with a text from Everly to confirm that she was on it, and she was sending someone this evening to take the computers. He followed Finnley out.

She stood in the middle of the store as if she was lost. She had to be feeling gutted right now, and maybe his questions had taken her down a road she'd never traveled.

He led her up the stairs and into the apartment. "I'll make us some dinner. We can talk, or we can sit in silence. Whatever you need. It's a lot to take in." He hoped she would open up and tell him more, much more. She probably knew plenty and didn't even realize it. But he wouldn't press her.

"I'm going to go downstairs and secure everything. Lock up. Then I'll be right back."

He was grateful for the excuse to put space between them. His heart was breaking for all that she was going through, and he could not afford to become this emotionally attached. What was wrong with him? Maybe it was because Caine knew a special person when he saw one, and he would do everything… *everything* in his power to protect her and to find the truth.

"I won't let you down."

God, please, I can't let her down.

While Caine checked on things below, Finnley moved to her bedroom and stared at the crumpled bed she'd failed to make in days. What did it matter? She felt numb all over—her mind's defenses kicking in—but that didn't mean she didn't want to climb into her bed and curl into a ball and sleep forever.

God, please. I want to wake up from this nightmare!

But this wasn't a nightmare. This was real, and she didn't want Caine to see her completely collapse. She had to stay strong to see this through. For Dad. She didn't want to depend on Caine either, but…

What would I do without him?

In her private bathroom, she splashed water on her face and brushed her hair. She could at least look like she was holding it together. She and Dad both signed the lease on the shop and the apartment. He'd claimed it was in case anything happened to either of them. Basically, he had no estate and there was nothing to will to her that she didn't already have her name on.

She grabbed her Bible off the side table and moved back into the living room, flipping on all the lights. It was still daylight, but evening would settle in soon and make the apartment entirely too dark. Finnley needed to read her Bible. She needed to read words that would soothe her soul.

Please, God…

Settling onto the sofa, she held the Bible to her chest and closed her eyes.

Lord, I feel betrayed. She drew in a few breaths.

She opened her eyes, searched through a few pages until she landed in the book of Psalms and slipped on her earbuds to listen to praise music.

"The Lord is nigh unto them that are of a broken heart; and saveth such as be of a contrite spirit." Psalm 34:18.

Finnley opened her eyes to find Caine crouched in front of her. His smile was soft and tender.

Realizing she'd fallen asleep, she pulled out her earbuds. She noticed the blanket draped around her and that her Bible was now on the table.

"I'm sorry I woke you, but I thought you might like something to eat while it's hot."

He stood and walked to the small dining table and held a chair out for her. He was taking care of her, doing more than he should do for his job. She got the feeling that he didn't mind. Finnley sat at the table and let him push her chair forward.

She didn't mind that either.

The aroma of beef stroganoff brought her fully awake. Caine had somehow learned of her favorite food and cooked it for her. He sat across from her now.

Eager.

Waiting.

Could he be any more thoughtful? She held his gaze and tried to read in his eyes why he would do this. But she didn't find answers. Still, she found compassion.

"Thank you," she whispered.

"You're welcome. Now, eat up."

She wasn't hungry, but Caine was trying to take care of her, and maybe she needed to eat. He'd made her favorite food. How could she refuse? Maybe she was reading too much into this. After all, he probably found the dried mushrooms in the pantry. The sour cream would go bad if he didn't use it, and all the rest he needed was in the freezer or pantry. Even if Caine hadn't known, God knew.

They ate in comfortable silence for a few minutes. She didn't want to talk about herself or her father or her life, so before Caine could bring any of that up, she said, "Tell me your story, Caine. Your life. Where you grew up. Where you went to school. What you did before working with your siblings, or have you always worked in this business with them?"

His hazel eyes grew wide, and he just stared at her as if caught off guard. As if surprised she would care enough to ask. Or was it something else? Like he kept his private life to himself, and she'd overstepped by asking. Their partnership was a business partnership, after all.

"There's nothing much to tell. I was in the army stationed in Italy. After I came home, I went to work with Ayden. End of story."

Wow. For someone who liked to ask a lot of personal questions about her life, he wasn't very forthcoming about his own. Of course, he was only doing his job, but she expected more from him. If her past boyfriends had been more talkative, she might have learned the truth faster. In Caine's case, she got the feeling he just didn't like talking about himself.

Still, she would try.

"How about someone special? Surely a guy like you has someone in his life." She shouldn't have asked, but she realized she really wanted to know. Because if he did, then maybe he shouldn't be staying with her, helping her, looking at her like he wanted to know her better. Or was she imagining it? Had she lost her mind in this search for answers since her father's death. Her mind was searching for a way out and had found Caine.

Attractive.

Thoughtful and caring.

He pushed food around on his plate, putting her off. Her heart pounded. He was married, wasn't he? Finnley needed an answer.

"Caine?"

She might have said his name a little too forcefully, because his face jerked up to hers, and she saw guilt in his eyes.

Guilt!

She stopped breathing. Please let the answer be no. To think she'd let her thoughts wonder about this man who could very well be married. Even if he wasn't married, she had no right to let herself think about him in those terms. But right now, she was so emotionally vulnerable that her carefully placed walls had fallen. She kept thinking about how it felt to be in his arms. And that disturbed her.

Her life was a complete dumpster fire at the moment.

He blew out a resigned breath and slid his plate to the side. She'd ruined their meal with her question.

"There was someone special once," he said. "But she died."

An awkward silence lingered between them.

She didn't miss the slight crack in his voice. She shoved past the emotion thickening in her throat. "I'm sorry. I didn't mean to pry... I stepped over a line."

He pursed his lips and stared at his plate. "Sophie was everything to me. I met her in Italy. She died in a hit-and-run..." His expression hardened, but pain filled his eyes. "I saw the whole thing."

Caine stood and took his plate to the kitchen. "There's dessert when you're ready."

His tone told her everything—their moment, their connection, was gone.

She'd ruined it.

SEVEN

Finnley had insisted on cleaning up the dishes. Caine had planned to do it all, but he wouldn't fight her on it. Maybe she needed to occupy her mind.

He certainly did after her questions about his life and her statement.

Surely a guy like you has someone in his life.

And then he'd gone and mentioned Sophie. He'd opened himself up a little too much. Caine wanted to kick something.

Be professional, dude!

But he'd *wanted* her to know. Why? Why did he want her to know?

He was glad that she'd turned in early after finishing the dishes. She needed the rest, and he needed the space to get his head together. For their dessert, he'd found a couple of packages of instant chocolate pudding—nothing fancy—but it remained untouched in the fridge. He wasn't sure what had come over him, why he'd gone out of his way to make a nice dinner.

The protection detail contract didn't include emotional protection, and the physical protection referred to preventing someone from causing physical harm. It wasn't in his job description to make sure she ate and kept her strength up.

Any reasonable person would see what needed to be done, and Caine was more than a reasonable person in this case. He was emotionally involved. He knew he was in trouble the moment he'd first looked into those big brown eyes back in Ayden's office. Now that he was getting to know her, had watched the tilt of her face when she was thinking, the fire in her eyes when she got angry at him, the fear that seemed to take over her entire body at times, the grief and regret—Caine couldn't help but be drawn to her, to care about her. He had an up close and personal look at her very open and vulnerable heart every day.

He felt like he was quickly losing this battle. She'd suffered a major loss in her life. He got that. He still felt completely gutted at losing Sophie to her father's enemies. Finnley had found her father murdered. Caine had witnessed Sophie's murder—she'd been intentionally hit by a car. He'd held her in his arms as she'd died.

That shared experience of losing someone seemed to reach across the small distance between their hearts and pull them closer.

Much closer.

So he was even more sensitive to the fact that Finnley was looking pale and fragile. Every day, they discovered something new and devastating about her deceased father, a man she loved and admired. All of it was weighing on her. And therefore, weighing on Caine.

And that's why he'd ignored Everly's repeated calls and instead texted her that he was busy and would get back to her.

If he talked to Everly now, she would be able to tell that Caine was getting too emotionally connected to Finnley. She would be able to hear it in his voice.

Maybe.

But he wouldn't risk that happening.

Because he *was* too emotionally connected to Finnley.

Whatever.

The doors were all locked and the cameras set, and he had his computer on. He could monitor all the possible entrances on the outside and inside. Alarms would go off. They were safe for tonight. Of course, that was relative in multiple ways. Right now, it didn't feel like either of their hearts were safe.

Her question about being in a relationship clued him in that she'd been thinking along the same lines as he had—romantically. He couldn't let that happen, but how did he stop it?

Regardless of their emotional vulnerabilities, her physical safety—which was his priority right now—depended on how bad someone wanted to get to her.

He scratched his head as he paced and glanced at his phone and computer and out the windows repeatedly. His biggest question in all this was why would someone want to get to her? Did Finnley know something? Did she possess something they wanted? Maybe she didn't realize she knew wanted information.

Stranger things had happened.

Apparently, Everly had finally given up on calling him and sent him an email detailing that the computers had been handed off to a local forensics lab that also worked with law enforcement. They should have some answer soon, if those answers could be found on Frank's computer. Right now, Caine was even wondering if Frank was his real name. He'd searched through various databases but had come up empty. He wasn't as good as Everly. Finding something on Frank would be helpful. Then again, it could mean more pain for Finnley.

Yawning, Caine glanced at his watch—1:30 a.m. Caine moved to peer out the windows and glance up and down the street.

He froze. Someone stood in the alley again like before. Was he or she watching? Waiting? Caine slowly let the curtain back and moved to Finnley's bedroom door and knocked lightly. He hated to wake her, but he had to warn her.

She opened the door, her hair askew. "Caine, what's wrong?"

"I need to check on something outside. Stay here in your room with the door locked. Don't come out for any reason."

She pushed past him into the living room. She sat on the sofa where Caine had been sitting and looked at his open computer. "I'll watch the cameras on your computer, then I'll know if I'm in danger."

"Lock the door behind me, okay?"

She nodded and followed him down the stairs. He could watch all the cameras with his watch as well. No one was at the back door. He slipped out and then heard the lock engage. He crept around into the dark alley, leading with his gun, and went around behind another building before crossing the street to come up behind the watcher.

Caine crept up behind the man. Aimed his gun at him. "Hold it right there."

The man stiffened.

"Lift your hands up slowly where I can see them."

The man did as Caine asked.

"What are you doing out here?"

He said nothing.

"Turn around so I can see your face."

He didn't turn. Great. Not like Caine could shoot him in the back, nor could he arrest the man or cuff him. Legally, that is, unless it was a citizen's arrest, but on what charges? The guy wasn't talking, obviously not wanting Caine to hear his voice.

"Fine." *Let's see how he reacts to my next words.* "I'm calling the police."

The man suddenly took off running. Caine chased him, but the man disappeared down another alley. Caine wanted to give chase and get answers, but he'd already left Finnley alone longer than he'd intended. He ran back around to the building. The security light in front suddenly went off.

Not good. He called the police and raced toward the store. Finnley would have to let him in, but if the lights were off, that couldn't be good. That could mean someone had messed with the security system. Someone who was very good and knew what they were doing.

He sprinted to the store and tried the front door. Locked. He raced around the back to try that door. It was unlocked.

His heart dropped to his gut.

Heart pounding, Finnley breathed too hard. Too loud.

Now was the time to hold her breath, but all she could do was gasp as fear tried to strangle her.

The power had gone out, along with the cameras. She thought Caine had explained they weren't dependent on electricity and had batteries in case of a power failure. And the security system? He'd also warned her that a determined and knowledge-able person could overcome his efforts. Nothing was foolproof.

She dropped to the floor and crawled toward the bedroom. Initially, he'd told her to stay in the room and lock the door, but she'd insisted on watching the cameras and had counted on those to keep her safe. But the screens had suddenly gone blank, and then the power had gone out and left her in the dark. Not even the security light outside had been unaffected.

She stopped mid crawl when she heard a noise. Someone was in the room with her. She held her breath this time, but all she could hear was her pulse in her ears.

Was it Caine?

No. Caine would call out to her and make his presence known. She could even picture him running through the apartment searching for her. Someone else, someone dangerous and bent on harming her had entered her home. Why else would they cut the power and knock out the camera feed?

Where was Caine? Was he injured? Had he been taken out too? She wanted to scream, but that would only give her lo-cation away.

Finnley was afraid if she moved, she would be discovered.

She feared that even her wildly pounding heart might draw the intruder's attention. If only she could see something. The heavy light-blocking drapes coupled with the power outage had turned the apartment completely dark. She waited for her eyes to adjust, but there was simply no light whatsoever. She couldn't even make out the furniture. She needed to see the intruder.

She slowly let out a breath, quietly drew in another and heard breathing. Not hers.

Goose bumps crawled over her. Her arms and legs trembled, making it hard to remain perfectly still or to support herself since she remained in the crawl position.

Caine, where are you?

Lord, please help me!

The sound of movement drew her attention to the left and across the room. There was a grunt and scuffle. Caine! Maybe it was the wrong thing to do, but she used her cellphone and lit up the living room. Caine and the intruder wrestled over a gun.

Caine!

The intruder straddled Caine and turned the pistol to Caine's face.

What do I do? What do I do? She needed to find a way to help. There was a lamp over near the two fighting men. She could knock it over his head. Give Caine a chance. She started for the lamp.

The two men groaned with their efforts. She had to help Caine before it was too late.

Caine angled his eyes toward her, as if trying to send her a message, but she couldn't understand.

"Run, Finnley. Get out of here!" He growled out the words.

The intruder suddenly turned in her direction and aimed his gun at her. The sound of gunfire blasted though the apartment. Finnley dropped her phone and darkness fell again. Had she been shot? She felt no pain. She searched for her cell, found it and turned on the light.

Caine rammed into the intruder, who had almost made it to Finnley, and once again, the two fought. He must have knocked the gun out of the man's hand, or else Finnley would be dead.

She should do what he said and run, and maybe that would draw the attacker away from Caine.

And to her? She couldn't fight him off. She found the will to do what she had to do. The strength. The man had Caine in a headlock.

She found the gun and aimed it. "Stop or I'll shoot!"

He slowly released Caine. Sirens rang out. Then he jabbed his elbow into Caine's gut. Caine bent over in pain, and the man raced down the steps.

"Finnley, get somewhere safe!" Caine shouted and bounded down the steps after him.

Finnley hadn't shot the intruder, and the guy had preferred to take the chance that she wouldn't, and he'd run. She couldn't shoot him in the back and stop him. She wasn't even sure she could have actually pulled the trigger, but she wanted to learn to protect herself. Once she picked up her gun after the required time for the background check, she would take a course and get a concealed carry permit.

Her hands shook and her legs wobbled. Using her cell for light again, she found her way into the bedroom, opened the closet door and sat on the floor, holding the gun. She'd hired Caine to protect her, after all, and if she made herself a target, she was only distracting him from doing his job.

God, please help Caine.

Images of the two men fighting bombarded her mind. Both appeared to be well trained. The way he fought, the intruder must have been military or special forces as well. That was only a guess on her part. She'd never seen that kind of fighting or any kind of actual fighting up close and personal.

It left her shaken.

That, and thinking about how close she and Caine had both come to death.

The light suddenly came back on. Heavy footfalls pounded up the stairwell—multiple people were coming. Good guys or bad guys? Finnley didn't know.

She aimed the gun at the closet door.

"Finnley. It's me, Caine. Are you in here?"

"Yes! I'm here!" She set the gun aside and stood as the door swung open.

EIGHT

Finnley jumped into his arms as if he were a lifeline.

Caine wrapped his arms around her. "I've got you."

I've got you.

She'd been so brave trying to protect him and aiming to shoot the man who'd broken in. The man who'd aimed that same weapon at her and tried to shoot and kill her. He'd been wearing night-vision goggles, but Caine had spotted the intruder and immediately tackled the man before he'd taken a shot at Finnley, who'd crouched on the floor. She'd stopped crawling, hadn't seen the death shot coming. He didn't think he even had the heart to tell her how close to death she'd come.

Caine should never have let things get this far. Should never have put her in that position to be running for her life. At least she was safe now, for the moment. The sheriff's deputy stood at the door to her bedroom waiting on Caine and Finnley. Caine released Finnley and held her at arm's length.

Her big brown eyes stared back at him. "Did you get him?" she asked.

"No." Caine sagged under the weight of guilt. "There were two men. I couldn't leave you alone to chase after the one."

As it was, he should never have left the apartment to begin with. Maybe the man in the alley was only there to draw him out so the other intruder could enter. He wouldn't fall for that again.

"It's time to talk to the deputies and tell them what happened here. Are you ready?" he asked.

She nodded and lifted a gun by the grip, holding it between her two fingers and letting it dangle. "Take this please. It belonged to him."

Deputy Wayne seemed surprised. He acquired a plastic evidence bag and placed the gun inside.

Caine led them out to the living room and shared what had happened with Deputy Wayne, who wrote everything down, his eyebrows raised the entire time as though it was hard to believe. The small town of Emmons hadn't seen this type of crime.

"I'm hoping that with this attack, your sheriff will finally be willing to open up the case into Frank Wilbanks's death." Caine eyed Finnley. Maybe he should have made the request in private.

"I'll pass this on to Sheriff Henderson. And what's your relationship with Finnley?"

"She hired me to protect her while I also investigate."

Deputy Wayne looked between the two of them. "Protect her from what?"

Finnley stood, fisting her hands at her side. Uh-oh. Deputy Wayne had said the wrong thing. Caine didn't get how the guy could be so dense. Or maybe he wanted to hear Finnley tell him. But seriously? This was the wrong time.

"Your department has the report I filed before about someone running me off the road. Deputy Knowles found me hiding in the woods. My car was totaled, and I was scared they would come down to finish the job."

"And I filed a report about the attack after the funeral," Caine added.

"Someone is lurking around my apartment. And tonight, someone broke in and tried to kill me. I had to hire someone to investigate and protect me because you aren't doing your job. Because Sheriff Henderson isn't taking the threat seriously."

Finnley's face had turned red, and she looked like she might say more.

"All right. I'm sorry about what you've been through. I'll bring this to the sheriff's attention and see about opening the case once more. I can understand your frustration. We have one county detective who is pulled in a lot of directions, but I'll have a conversation with him as well." He glanced around the apartment. "In the meantime, I suspect she'll want us to gather evidence. This is a crime scene now. You'll need to find somewhere else to stay at least for the next twenty-four hours."

"What? You didn't kick me out when my father was murdered."

"It's my understanding that he committed suicide, and we didn't kick you out because we were able to gather the evidence we needed to rule out any other cause of death."

"This is a good thing, Finnley. We want to give them time and space to gather evidence. Getting DNA on the guy who was here could be the big break we need." Caine could easily see that Finnley was fuming. "All right, Deputy Wayne," he said. "I'll take care of getting us to another place."

He wrapped an arm around Finnley, who was now visibly trembling with anger. Caine pushed his own outrage down, but he had a good feeling about this deputy, especially if he was going to talk to the county detective. Caine might even pay him a visit as well.

He needed to keep a professional appearance and work well with the local law enforcement no matter his frustration at times. But often, this was why Honor Protection Specialists were hired, to supplement an investigation or dig deeper when clients weren't happy with the lack of answers.

He suspected the sheriff's department would now look closely at all aspects of the attacks on Finnley and likely open up a case file, if they didn't already have one since her father's death had been ruled a suicide from the start.

"I was moving us anyway," he whispered to Finnley. "Let's go pack up a few items in your room."

"Just a few," the deputy said. "We need to check everything."

Caine would take his computer without mentioning it to the officers, because the investigators didn't need it. He didn't want to cause an issue by even bringing it up.

Finnley sniffled, but she tried to hide her tears of anger and grief. Tonight had been a shock—for Caine too, honestly.

He assisted her in packing a few items and then turned to face the deputy who approached to make sure nothing more was taken. More deputies arrived, stomping around inside the apartment, downstairs in the shop and outside the building. Of course, messing up the "crime scene" they sought to protect.

"Finnley, hurry up. You can come back to get more later, but let's get out of here so law enforcement can do their job."

She'd changed into jeans and a T-shirt in the bathroom and slung a small bag over her shoulder. Caine moved to grab his luggage and quickly slipped his computer inside. They headed downstairs and out the front door of her father's shop and were met with the flashing lights of county sheriff's vehicles. Several deputies were having a discussion. Did they send the entire county out here?

Caine wanted to get away before they had to answer more of the same questions.

"Where are we going?" she asked.

"I've been working on a plan with Everly. We just have to move up the timeline. I had hoped not to have to use this, but I'm glad it was in the works."

Finnley's head was spinning, and her heart was beating double time. The county vehicles parked in the streets drew unwanted attention to her father's store and possibly his legacy. Though perhaps his supposed suicide had already done that. She didn't like this. Not one bit. In fact, she hated what was happening to her life.

Those thoughts soon fled as she realized that Caine was leading her down dark alleys and behind buildings, keeping to the shadows. Finnley didn't like his stealth movements and hiding as if they were criminals.

What was there to like about any of it.

What if they ran into one of the men? Wasn't this exactly from where the man or men had been watching her? A thousand questions flooded her mind, adding to the agitation that had started hours before when they'd discovered the hidden room.

But she was alive, and she had to keep trusting Caine, even though at this moment, she didn't understand what he was doing or where he was leading them. She guessed they were sticking to the shadows to protect her, but she realized they hadn't gone all that far when he stopped. Carrying their duffels, they'd simply walked a couple of blocks before disappearing around the back of the building and into the side of the building that was right across the street from Wilbanks & Co. and her apartment.

The building was now all part of a crime scene surrounded with what looked like the entire sheriff's department, though she knew that couldn't be true. Sheriff Henderson wasn't about to devote too much time to Finnley's situation. Still, maybe now the sheriff would finally dig deeper and believe Finnley.

From her hiding place, she stared across the street at the emergency vehicles. The flashing lights. It all drew attention to the shop.

Again.

It reminded her of finding Dad with a gunshot to the head. She blinked back the sudden surge of tears.

You didn't kill yourself. I knew it. I knew you would never deliberately leave me.

With attacks on her now ramping up, maybe they would look into her father's death again and find what she'd known all along. Caine finally opened the side entrance into the building, and they stepped quietly up the back stairwell. The place seemed dark and empty and creepy, and he shined a flashlight as they walked. Caine had a way about him that chased the fear away. She was safe while she was with him.

Together, they crept down the long, dark hallway. "Caine, where are we going?" she whispered. No one was around, so she wasn't sure why talking in a normal voice seemed inappropriate under their current cloak-and-dagger methods.

"I'll explain everything," he whispered.

She definitely would never usually be inside this building at night alone. Of course, she wouldn't be here at all if Caine hadn't led her here. He flashed the beam across doors as they passed and then finally stopped in front of one. Pausing as if trying to decide if he was in the right place.

Or in his right mind.

"This has to be it," he whispered and lowered his duffel to the floor.

Tired of lugging it around, she did the same.

Caine handed her a small flashlight. "Hold this, would you?"

She took it.

He knelt next to the door. "Shine it here, please."

She shined it at the doorknob and watched him work the lock without a key. "What are you doing?"

He continued to struggle but didn't answer.

"Are you breaking in? I thought you said—"

"Keep your voice down, Finnley." His voice was so low she almost couldn't hear. "We don't want anyone to know we're here."

Fine. She'd whisper her incredulity. "You're breaking in. This isn't legal. I can't be part of this."

The door creaked open. Caine led with his gun and slipped inside, pulling her behind him. He shut the door and pressed his back against a wall, as did she.

Heart pounding, she held her breath. *What are we doing?* But she followed his lead and kept quiet. They dropped their duffels to the floor. He took back the small flashlight he'd given her and made quick work of clearing the space as she stuck right next to him. He moved to the windows that were completely covered with shades as well as dark curtains to block out the light. He checked those, and then flipped on the small lamp on a table next to a sofa.

Finnley released her pent-up breath.

Caine blew out a breath as if he'd held his too. "Everly had already secured this place for us. The keys were on their way. Should arrive tomorrow."

"So it's an apartment?" Surprised, Finnley glanced around the spacious place. "I had no idea this existed above Ye Olde Antique Shop. I figured Gerry stored stuff up here."

"Neither did I, but I told Everly my plans and she found this. Couldn't be more perfect."

"Perfect? I don't get it. Why did you move us right across the street. How is that perfect or safer?"

"Well, no one is expecting us to be here of all places. But it will be a few days before the intruders return to your place since the sheriff's department is there collecting evidence for the foreseeable future. That's good and bad."

"What could be bad about that?"

"I intended to use this apartment to surveil. I'm expecting more tech tomorrow, including a drone. I had hoped to follow the watcher with the drone and find out who he is. I sent the picture I caught of the guy in the woods to Everly, but it just wasn't enough to give us anything. She's sending it to a specialist to see if he can enhance it so we can use it to learn the identity of those behind the attacks."

"And behind killing my father."

His lips pressed together, and he looked at her eyes. Was it her imagination, or had his gaze dropped to her mouth? Her heart rate shot up again, especially when he stepped closer and took both her hands into his.

"Yes. We'll find whoever is behind your father's murder, and now, with the sheriff's department on board, we'll figure things out faster. I hope. In the meantime, nothing is more important than your safety."

She chuckled at that. "Right. Apparently, following the watcher is more important."

"This from the woman who told me she wasn't ready to move to a safer location? I'm trying to juggle many things here. Investigate. Protect. And, yes, keep my client happy." He grinned, and she was sure it was to take the edge off his words.

His grin was a big part of his charm, and he pulled her right in with that. She might believe anything he told her. That might make him dangerous.

"Okay. I get it. You figured out how to keep me close and 'safe' while also watching to see who would come for me. We're going to watch the watchers."

He grinned again, then his expression turned serious. "Someone will return because they could think you're still there. And this time, I'll be ready."

"So am I working at the shop during the day?"

"Yes. I'll be with you. I'll put the lights in the apartment above on timers to coincide with the normal rhythms of someone staying there even when we aren't, and then we'll find a way to slip out and back into *this* apartment."

He still held her hands, and tenderness poured from his eyes. Her heart beat erratically, and she wanted to step away, but she couldn't make her body comply. He released her right hand and gently brushed her hair from her cheek with his left. The gentle touch of his fingers sent tingles over her.

What am I going to do? Was she being the fool again? And if so, that could only lead to one end, and she couldn't bear to have her heart broken a third time. But Caine's charm, grin, good looks and compassion were so hard to resist. But she had to find a way.

After her father's death, she was already shattered, and she didn't need Caine to spread the shattered pieces into the wind.

NINE

A few days later, Caine was surprised that no one had showed up to surveil Finnley. He grew antsy waiting. They had figured out a system of working at the shop. Caine had programmed timers for the lights and television to come on and go off so it looked like they were inside. He was still able to use the cameras at the old apartment and shop to watch the alley on this side, because he couldn't easily see someone watching the place from across the street.

So far, he couldn't see anyone watching them during the daytime, so this was all about being ready at night. He decided that the reason someone had watched at night was to draw him out and away from Finnley.

Well, he wasn't falling for that again. However, he didn't put it past these criminals to try again.

Go ahead. Watch us at night. See what happens.

Ready and waiting for action, the drone sat on the table unpacked and assembled, but there was no one to watch or follow. The discovery of computers in the hidden room hadn't yielded any intel, and, at the moment, his only real hope for a break in this case was that the sheriff's department had come across DNA in the store or the apartment that would give them meaningful leads.

Maybe the county sheriff had made that discovery, but they had not shared the information with Caine. Sheriff Henderson was still unconvinced that Finnley's father had been murdered. The scenario she suggested was more hurtful to Finnley, who sat curled on the sofa reading her Bible.

Hadn't she been through enough?

He thought back to their conversation in the sheriff's department, when she'd called them both in to ask more questions about the incident and the break-in.

She'd come to talk to them both in an interview room after they'd been questioned separately, and she'd invited Detective Wilson. Caine wasn't a fan of her tactics at all.

"Finnley, I'm still not convinced your father was murdered. Someone has clearly targeted you, or perhaps some information they think you have, something you know *because* of your father. This could be the very reason he committed suicide, because of some crime that he committed or someone he wronged that was coming for him."

While her theories weren't off track, she could have worded them much better.

Finnley had been in too much shock after the sheriff's "theories," so Caine had spoken on her behalf.

"We still maintain that he was murdered, and we're requesting another autopsy performed by an another medical examiner."

That should have been done to begin with.

"And that's your prerogative." The sheriff had almost glared at them both...almost, but not quite... "You'll need to petition to exhume the body." She passed her lips into a thin line. "You're free to go." Sheriff Henderson turned to walk out.

"Uh, Sheriff, I'd like to talk to Finnley some more," Detective Wilson said.

"I have another meeting, so take it from here." Sheriff Henderson exited the room.

Caine got the distinct impression that the sheriff didn't like Finnley. Anyone in the room would have gotten that impression. He decided she was unprofessional, but he didn't know what kind of pressure she was under. He knew all too well from experience working with law enforcement that there could be some other crisis taking all her time, relegating the Wilbanks suicide/murder and Finnley's attacks to the back burner.

Detective Wilson flipped his iPad open to stare at his notes. "I agree getting another autopsy is important, but considering you'll need to exhume the body, let's hope there's another way to get to the truth. The coroner, McFarland, is committed to his stance that your father committed suicide." He skimmed through a couple of pages and then said, "I want all the facts you can share. This case was only recently handed off to me." Wilson looked up from the iPad and leaned in. "Finnley, you need to think hard about what your father could have been involved in, or what reason anyone would have to target you." His eyes flicked to Caine and held a steely glint. "And if you're going to hire protection, make sure he does the job."

Ah. Caine was just beginning to like this guy. But to be fair, the detective wasn't wrong, and Caine would hold his judgment.

"I… I don't know anything." She rubbed her forehead. "I'll keep trying to think of something, anything I could have missed."

"Fair enough." Wilson stood and dropped a card on the table. "That has my cell number. Call if you think of anything. Night or day. Either of you."

Finnley slid the card toward her. "Thank you, Detective Wilson."

He nodded and walked out.

Every time Caine thought back to the sheriff's attitude toward Finnley, anger burned in his gut. And the sheriff wasn't wrong about Finnley being targeted. Finnley had nearly been taken out while Caine had been busy chasing after someone who'd been watching them. It was hard to hide in a small town like this.

Finnley yawned. "I think I'm going to bed, Caine."

"All right. Sleep tight."

He watched her walk down the short hallway to her new temporary bedroom. How long would he keep them here, living in a place that didn't belong to her while they waited for answers?

The truth was, they might never get answers.

His cell buzzed with a call from Everly. He texted her, requesting that she text back so he wouldn't disturb Finnley.

Everly texted:

Frank's computer drive was wiped. He must have known something was coming down, and he did it himself.

Caine responded: Great, what next?

Everly replied:

I'll employ some special techniques to see if we can still recover the data. And if I can't do it, I know a guy who knows a guy.

Caine replied:

Just do your thing, Everly. The sheriff's department has a detective who is looking into things too. Maybe I should have told Detective Wilson about the computer.

Everly:

I've documented everything, and we'll maintain the chain of custody, but when you were hired, this wasn't an open investigation. The sheriff and her detective will appreciate the help when we give her something.

Everly had been a police officer for the Tacoma PD before transitioning to Honor Protection Specialists, and she kept on top of all she learned, bringing it with her to their company.

Caine typed another message as he peered out the crack in the curtain. Anything else?

Everly replied: Yes.

A figure moved in the shadows. Bingo! Caine generated a text by voice:

Wait a minute. Hold it. The watcher is back. I'm on it.

Be careful out there.

Caine could hardly believe it. Finally. His patience had paid off. Caine grabbed the drone. Now the trick would be to get the guy to flee again, and Caine would use the drone to follow him without leaving this apartment.

Just how am I going to do that? He knew just the thing. He called 911 and reported someone watching the apartment again, and to let Detective Wilson know too. He didn't want a repeat of what had happened the other night when Finnley was almost shot and killed.

They might respond or they might not, since someone wasn't actually breaking in, but given the recent small-town crime wave involving Wilbanks & Co., he hoped they would take quick action. Once that county vehicle drove up, the man watching the shop would probably leave, and Caine would follow with the drone.

He focused on getting the drone ready. Prior to this evening, he had removed the window screen, and he would only need to quietly open the window. All he had to do was fly the drone out the window and follow from a distance.

And now…to wait for the guy to leave.

Caine glanced at his watch and waited for the sheriff's department. Five minutes passed. *This is ridiculous. Do I need to call them again and maybe say someone broke in?*

That would be a lie, and he would get in trouble.

A sheriff's county vehicle finally pulled up in front of the shop, lights flashing, but no sirens.

Phew.

Caine sent the drone out the window and high into the sky to watch from a distance. Sure enough, the watcher fled down the alley. Caine viewed the images on the screen as the drone followed, keeping a distance so it wouldn't be heard or discovered. He'd made sure to secure a top-notch camera so he could watch from a long distance and catch good video and photos. Technology was always improving, and he was pleased with himself. Well, Everly had played a huge role in getting the right equipment—that was her job—but he'd made the request and the plan.

The man kept to the shadows and fled to a Chevy Tahoe parked behind a building three blocks down on the outskirts of town. He slowly drove away as if making sure to avoid the cop car. Caine took a picture of the license plate with the drone and continued to follow for several miles until the vehicle moved out of the range of the drone and the camera. Caine flew the drone back and was careful to guide it into the window.

He wished he could have followed the man to his home, his hideout, his lair, whatever, but at least he had a license place. Now they were getting somewhere.

The next morning, Finnley and Caine spoke with Everly over the speakerphone, making a plan for Finnley's schedule at the shop. Mr. Patel, a neighboring shopkeeper, could help her take time off.

"I'm sure we can trust him, Caine," Finnley said.

"I'm sure too," Everly said over the speakerphone.

Caine stared at his computer.

"Dad had to take a break now and then, and Mr. Patel is someone we've known forever. He knows the store. He's fine. He isn't involved with any bad guys."

"Maybe it isn't safe for him." Caine lifted his gaze to Finnley. "What about *his* safety?"

"I concur with Caine," Everly said. "You can trust him, but we don't know what's going on and who's coming at you."

Finnley's throat grew tight. "I don't want to close the store. At the same time, I don't want to lose customers." Rubbing her arms, she walked around the apartment that wasn't hers. This was all so surreal.

"The Wilbanks & Co. store has been around for a long time and has loyal customers," Everly said. "In fact, it might be a good idea to post a sign on the door, announcing you're changing up the times the store is open. Work two days a week, or three, if you have to. Or nothing at all. You won't lose customers."

Everly was nice to reassure her, but Finnley wasn't sure. "I don't know."

"Look, this isn't an everyday situation," Caine said. "Once this is over, you can get back to your normal life."

"If you want," Everly said, "I can help craft a letter to your customers. You have the addresses all tucked away in a hardbound book."

"As opposed to the computer." Finnley stopped pacing and stared at Caine's phone. "I get it. I can write the letter. That will give me something to do if I can't be at the store."

"Look, Finnley." Caine stood, gently gripped her arms and then slid his hands down to hers. Chills—the good kind—crawled up her arms. "This might just be a morning excursion to the address to which the vehicle is registered. We can't know that it will take all day. Just keep the Closed sign in place. It's going to be fine. People will understand. You've been through a tragedy."

"He's right," Everly said. "Some people would take days off. Weeks away. While I think in a normal situation bringing in some help is a good idea, it's not good in this situation."

Finnley hung her head, and Caine fairly ducked to look up at her with a smile. His grin. *That* grin. How could he smile at a time like this? And yes, how could she *not* respond to him? She did. She totally smiled. "Okay. We'll just leave it closed until I get back."

"Good." He released her hands. "Grab your purse and a rain jacket and let's go."

"Over and out, Caine. Keep me posted on what's happening," Everly said.

"Will do." Caine seemed giddy.

Finnley tugged on her rain jacket and pulled her purse over her shoulder. She watched Caine while she did. "You like the action, don't you?"

"It's more fun than a stakeout, don't you think?"

"Maybe." He was rubbing off on her. She followed him out of their secret apartment, and they walked multiple back alleys to a parking lot where Caine climbed into a vehicle different than his 4Runner—a white Ford Escape—that sat in the parking lot behind the store. "This feels so cloak-and-dagger and makes me nervous."

"This is safe. All we're doing is going to the address and we'll watch."

"Why don't we just send the police to the address?"

"Based on what? I followed him home after I saw him in an alley? I need actionable evidence to get anywhere. That's what I'm hoping to get today." He started the Escape and pressed his hand against the console as he turned to back up. "There's a nice stakeout camera in the back."

"Kind of like what private investigators use to get incriminating photographs when someone is cheating?"

He huffed. "Just to be clear, I've never done that kind of a job." He entered the address and followed the prompts.

The place was forty-five minutes away.

On the drive, they kept to light and easy topics about likes and dislikes. He must have understood she'd been through so much lately and needed to feel like her world wasn't crumbling around her.

Finnley found that they had a lot in common. She preferred the mountains to the beach, as did Caine. She loved Italian food more than just about anything else, except maybe stroganoff. Caine's favorite was lasagna. She'd always wanted to ride horses. Turned out that Caine had a horse growing up. His parents had owned stables. But both of them were gone now, and that home had been sold along with the horses. She was getting to know him and liked what she'd learned so far.

She'd hired Caine, but she was starting to feel like he was much more than a bodyguard slash investigator. She had the sudden urge to reach across the console and hold his hand. Instead, she fidgeted.

Suddenly, Caine took her hand and held it. Had he done that to stop her from wringing her hands? Or had he done it because he'd read her mind or even felt the draw, the connection between them?

"Don't be nervous. It's going to be okay, Finnley. We're going to find out who killed your father."

She nodded, trusting his words, hoping in them. He misunderstood. Her nervousness had everything to do with him and nothing to do with their investigation, which told her that she was getting off base and growing too close to him despite her best efforts.

Still, once the investigation was over and Dad had justice and Finnley was safe, she would have no reason to see Caine again. Just as well.

Unfortunately, the thought left her unsettled.

Finally, he parked on the street.

"Which one is it?"

"Oh, I didn't park in front of it."

"I get it. That would be too obvious."

"And even here, neighbors can start to get suspicious."

"What happens then? Do they come out and talk to you and ask you what you're doing?"

"No. They usually call the police."

"Oh, so you've had this happen before?"

"Yep. Multiple times."

"So if the policeman approaches you, what does he say?"

"He asks me about my business, and I explain that I'm a private investigator and this is a public street. But usually, he or she will insist I move along."

"So that blows your stakeout?"

"Depends on where I'm parked and the neighbor who called. I usually just comply and move my car. That can happen a lot. But honestly, I don't conduct a lot of my investigations this way. Sometimes you just can't get around physical surveillance."

"So here we are."

"Yes. See the fourth house down to the right? That's the one registered to the vehicle the watcher took."

"I don't see the Tahoe, though."

"It could be in the garage. I'm going to do a slow drive-by." He steered forward, and they talked and looked straight ahead with brief glances to all the houses.

"Nope, not in the garage," she said. "It's filled with stuff. Looks like a bunch of kids with all those bikes."

In the rearview mirror, she spotted a family of five—mother, father and three kids—emerge from the home and pile into a minivan.

"I don't know what to think," she said. Her hopes were diving. "I can't believe that guy would be the one to slink around in the shadows or be involved in the attack on me. He has a family."

"Unfortunately, you'd be surprised. Outward appearances don't always tell the whole story. The Tahoe is registered to him, though."

"So where it is? Are we going to talk to them?"

"Not yet. Everly is looking at the father because we know it was a man. If this family guy is part of this, then we'll know."

"Are we sticking around to watch more?"

"No. I think we've seen enough." He contacted Everly and told her everything. "Sending you a picture."

Finnley jerked her head to him. "When did you take a picture?"

"This vehicle has a camera."

"You mean a dashcam like cops have."

"Similar."

"You guys think of everything, don't you?"

"We try, but we're only human." He glanced her way, shooting her that grin she was coming to love.

"I'm not finding anything about Thomas Dane, the man to which the vehicle is registered, that concerns me," Everly said. "Nor has the vehicle been reported stolen, so we need to find out what's going on. Since it's an older model, there's no integrated GPS or tracking, so I can't find it. I think you should turn around and talk to him."

"In front of his family?" Finnley asked. "What if he is involved?" She couldn't stand the thought of all of this unfolding in front of his kids, but then again, they needed to resolve this.

"Talk to him." Everly's tone didn't leave room for an argument.

TEN

Caine steered around the block, then turned into the drive as the vehicle was pulling out. Caine didn't want to block the minivan, so he pulled up and parked in front of the house. Then he jumped out and approached the driver's side before the man escaped with his family.

The man lowered the window. "What do you think you're doing?"

"Excuse me, Mr. Dane? I'm sorry to bother you," Caine said. "But can I have a word with you?"

A deep, angry frown formed on the man's face, then he quickly softened his features. His family was watching, after all. "I'm heading out with my wife and kids. What's this about?"

"If you don't mind, let's speak in private." Caine really wished he could have done this without the family present.

The man spoke a few words to his wife, then the window went up. He got out, and the doors locked. He walked with Caine to the end of the drive. "I need to talk to you about the Tahoe that's registered to you."

"What about it, and who are you?"

"I'm a private investigator with Honor Protection Specialists. We suspect your Tahoe is being used in criminal activity."

His eyes widened, and his face grew red. "What? That's impossible."

"Sir, where is the vehicle now?"

He roughed a hand down his face and then around the back of his neck while he took in the information. Formulating his response?

"My younger sister. I let her borrow it. Wait…" His chest rose and fell in panic, and then his shoulders sagged. "She's in Hawaii with her boyfriend. Could it have been stolen?"

"Possibly. Mind giving me the address. I'll drive by and see if I can locate it."

"Should I call the police? I'm calling the police." The man fished out his smartphone. While he was on hold with 911, he lifted his gaze to Caine. "You said you're a private investigator. Who are you working for again?"

"I'm with HPS—Honor Protection Specialists. I'm working for someone who is being targeted, was targeted by the man driving your Tahoe."

The guy stared at him, his eyes widening. Then he lifted his hands. "Whoa, whoa. That's not me. I wasn't driving."

"I believe you." This guy wasn't as tall or as buff. Caine had encountered him in the alley once and knew at least that much. He hadn't seen the face of the man in Finnley's apartment because he'd worn a mask.

Dane turned away as he reported the suspicious activity involving his sister's vehicle to the police. Finishing the call, he turned to Caine. "They're going to have an officer call me back."

"You'll have to file a report." Caine handed the guy his card. "I can drive by where you think the car should be, or you can let me know where it is."

"I think it's probably stolen, and therefore won't be there anyway. I don't feel comfortable giving you that information, but if you're an investigator, you can probably find it anyway."

Figured. "Thanks for your help."

Mr. Dane stared at Caine, clearly upset. He got on his cell again, and Caine suspected he was calling his sister now.

Well, that was a waste of energy. Caine strode to the Escape and got in with Finnley.

"Well?"

"The guy claims he loaned it to his sister and she's out of town." He called Everly and relayed all the information.

"I have her address. If you want to drive by the house, it's not ten minutes from where you are."

"She could have parked it at the airport," Finnley offered. "If they're on a trip."

"She's right," Caine said and steered away from the house. Mr. Dane and his family got out of the minivan and went back into the house.

Looked like Caine had just ruined their day.

All in a day's work...

He entered the address into the navigation system and steered away from the man's house. He followed the directions, feeling like he'd gained nothing and only frustrated a family.

Caine arrived at the house in just under ten minutes, and he drove slowly by.

"Well, it's not there, unless it's in the garage," Finnley said.

"Yep." He parked, hopped out and peeked into the garage. Not there. He got back in.

"Empty?" she asked.

He steered away from the house. "I wouldn't say that. It's filled with the stuff of life, but not the Tahoe."

"I guess that's probably a good thing."

"Why do you say that? If we found the vehicle and it wasn't stolen, then we'd have a lead on who is targeting you." Who killed your father.

"Yeah, maybe. But I saw the man and his family, and I don't like the idea of his sister or her boyfriend being involved and hurting that family."

Finnley never stopped being tenderhearted, did she? "You don't even know them."

"I don't have to know someone well to know that I like them."
She gave him a smile that went all the way to her big brown eyes.

That brilliant smile could undo him.

"So, what's next?" she asked.

"Let's get you back to the shop, unless you have another idea."

"No, that's a good one. Maybe I should do as Everly suggested, though, and cut back on the hours."

Caine wasn't sure how much business Wilbanks & Co. actually did in a year, but he noted that Saturdays, the weekends, were the busiest days. Despite his earlier observation that the store had no online presence, the place did well with a loyal customer base built over years. And, obviously, enough people came in—tourists especially—to have kept the business going for years.

A couple of hours later, Caine worked to reset the cameras. They kept glitching. Even though they were staying in the apartment across the street, he could still watch this place while they weren't here, but only if he could get things to work properly.

Finnley assisted a woman at the counter who'd bought some personal designs she'd ordered weeks ago. Designed by her father. Finnley explained deftly that her father had passed. When the woman left, Finnley moved to flip the Closed sign and lock the doors. She pressed her back against it.

"Are you okay?" Caine left the camera and backed down the ladder.

"Yes. I will be."

He moved to stand in front of her. "I know it was hard to talk about your father's death like that, but you did well. I'm impressed."

Pain flitted across her features before she moved to the register. "I need to close out, and then I'll be done. How long do we have to stay in the other apartment?"

"Until it's safe to come back here." Or until it's time to move somewhere else. Oh, he'd left the camera hanging. He needed to adjust it before he put the ladder away. He climbed back up and got busy while she continued to close out the register.

She probably wanted to know how long it would take him to find the men behind her father's death and bring her closure. How long he would need to protect her. In the end, this was costing her money.

"Caine?"

The way she said his name pulled his attention from the camera he'd adjusted. "What is it?"

From behind the counter, she lifted the keys. "These are the keys I use to lock the register."

He came down the ladder, folded it and set it against the wall to put away later, then he moved to her side.

"And?"

"I only need one key. What are all these other keys for? I never asked. But they must be for something."

Caine took the keys. "Padlock keys. I haven't seen anything here or upstairs in the apartment that was locked." He studied her. The use of a padlock was unlimited. Caine would think big to start. "Do you have any other property with a barn or a trailer, even? Could your dad have had a storage unit?"

Finnley stood outside the Emmons Budget Storage while Caine tried the key. She'd stopped in at the main office, where she caught a woman, Jessica, just locking up to leave for the day. Finnley explained her situation. Fortunately, Jessica had known her father, and that he'd recently died. She showed compassion and looked up Finnley's father's storage unit number, then she sent them on their way. Jessica mentioned she didn't contact Finnley about the storage because it was all paid up, so it wasn't flagged.

Finnley thanked Jessica, and Caine steered the vehicle slowly down the rows of storage units until they came to unit B-24. They had a key, after all—at least, she hoped they did.

And if the key didn't work in the padlock, they at least now knew her father had a storage unit. Caine could disable the padlock, he claimed, with or without the key.

Now they stood at the unit.

Suddenly, her entire body started shaking, and she hugged herself to hide her reaction to the unknown and yet another discovery. Was she truly prepared for what lay behind this door? She knew far too little about her father and his affairs. Right now, she would think of it as his affairs, his business dealings, whatever, that he'd thought Finnley was...what? Too young? Finnley tried to hold out hope that maybe her father would have told her everything at some point when he believed it was the right time. The man she'd known had been too good—too honest, even—to live a life of lies, in continual deception.

Finally, she felt herself calming down. She hadn't wanted Caine to see, but he probably had because he was trained to notice pretty much everything. Under normal circumstances, that could have been a good thing. But not here. Not now. Not for Finnley.

For that reason, it probably would have been better if she had gone into this alone, done the research on her own and investigated as much as she could on her own, then she wouldn't have to be concerned about someone else seeing her entire life crumble. Watching her fall apart.

But that wasn't really being fair to herself or to Caine. After all, she was *holding* it together because he was in this with her.

Drawing her focus to the present, he unlocked the padlock, removed it and turned to her. His hazel eyes were luminous as he studied her. He wouldn't open the floodgate of who knew what—not until she gave the word. He seemed to sense her moods and understand things she hadn't even voiced. How could such a tough guy be so sensitive to her needs? Maybe she was just imagining it, but it seemed like they were in tune.

"Are you ready?" he asked.

"No. I'll never be ready. But we still need to open this." She took a step forward and, with his help, rolled the door up to reveal what was inside the storage unit.

"Um… Maybe we should shut this." Caine stepped inside with Finnley and rolled the door shut behind them so they were in the dark, then he found a switch and flicked on the battery-powered light. "Looks like your father set it up as kind of an office away from an office so he could work in here. Power and everything."

On the walls were semiautomatic handguns, various kinds of rifles with complicated scopes, knives and more.

She couldn't stop staring. Her father, who didn't even use a smartphone, who avoided technology and hated guns…

Who are you?

Were…you?

"I don't get it," she said. "This can't belong to him." But she knew it did. The key had been hidden in plain sight. "I… What is any of this for? Who was he?"

Finnley sat in the chair in the corner while Caine took pictures and made notes in his phone. She really had to dig deeper to figure out who her father really was.

Unfortunately, that was leading to other, deeper questions.

Who am I?

She couldn't truly know who *she* was if her father wasn't who he said he was, could she?

Why didn't she question anything? Even her own life? She lived above the shop in an apartment with her father and worked with him and never dreamed of doing something more or different. Of the larger world outside Emmons, Washington. She'd been perfectly happy.

What was wrong with her? Because clearly her father had

more curiosity than she had. He'd lived a double life. And with that realization, she found herself wanting more. She just didn't know what.

But first things first. She had to find out about her father. Who he was and who killed him.

She hadn't realized she was lost in another world until Caine was crouching in front of her. "Are you all right?"

"No. I'm not. I won't ever be the same again."

"I'm so sorry, Finnley. Can I do anything? I mean, to help you. More than I'm doing now."

He referred to investigating and protecting her, of course.

"You can teach me to use a gun. I'm supposed to pick it up this week. I was going to take a course to get my concealed carry permit, but before that, I would really like to know how to even use it."

She caught the slightest of flinches, but he hid his surprise well and studied her long and hard. "We'll talk about this more later, but if you decide that's what you want, then I'm happy to help."

"I don't need to talk about it more. I've decided."

He stood. "Finnley, you're in shock, which is understandable. I know you bought a gun right after your father was killed. And that makes sense. You were scared. This isn't the time to make major decisions."

She stood too and perused her father's collection. "My father clearly knew how to shoot, and I want to know too."

"Why? Whatever this is, learning to shoot won't bring him back. Won't make you feel better. You don't need to prove yourself or make yourself like him. We don't even know who he really was."

"He lived a double life. I wonder if he was a spy or something. Maybe even a double agent." The words sounded farfetched when she spoke them, but then again…

By the way Caine pursed his lips, she knew that he had

wondered the same thing. Or he was still wondering and just waiting for answers.

"I wish you didn't have to see this. To go through this. Maybe it's time to let the sheriff's department handle the investigation."

"Do you really think they will follow through? They've let me down, Caine." She shoved away from him, anger burning in her gut that he would suggest it.

"I'm sorry. I was only thinking of you. What's best for you."

She drew in a fast breath, forcing the surge of tears back before she turned on him. "That's not up to you. Your job is to investigate and to protect me." She admitted that with her last words he hadn't strayed far from that task. "Protect me physically. You don't need to protect me emotionally."

Her words had the intended effect. He blinked and stepped back. She saw the moment the tenderness disappeared. He'd shuttered his emotions. She'd hurt him with the words, hurt herself as well. Deep inside, she wished she could allow herself to explore much more with him. Because more than anything, she wanted to lean into him and draw strength from him. But she knew better. She'd learned her lesson twice before. And right now, she needed to be strong on her own. Caine would move on to the next case, and she had no doubt he would be equally as endearing to the next client as he was to her.

She blinked back the stupid tears again. Finnley needed to reinvent herself because she had a feeling whatever she would face next would require a stronger, more resilient person. "So what do you make of all this?"

"I sent all the information about the storage unit and images to Everly. This is all evidence, and I'm trained to collect, but there could eventually be other agencies involved. I need to put a call in to Ayden to find out our next steps. This could be bigger than any of us thought, and we want to handle the evidence the right way, for your father's sake and for your protection."

His cell rang. "It's Everly."

He answered. "Yep."

"Get out of there, Caine," she said. "I don't think it's safe, and you could have been followed. This is much bigger than we thought. I'm consulting with local law right now."

"You mean Lincoln." Detective Lincoln Mann had been a strong ally to HPS in the past, and Everly had worked with him in the Tacoma PD.

"Yes. He advised you to leave."

"Right."

Caine had put Everly on speaker. Someone could be hiding and waiting. Cautiously, they slipped out. Caine turned, rolled the door back down and locked it. Bursts of gunfire suddenly filled the air. Bullets ricocheted off the door.

Fire lit her shoulder, and she screamed.

ELEVEN

Caine rushed Finnley forward and assisted her into the Escape, shielding her with his body and returning fire.

"Get down, Finnley. Stay down."

She'd been shot. He'd seen the blood. This was all on him. He shouldn't have taken her. He should have expected this would be dangerous and seen that someone had followed them.

Gunfire pinged the vehicle.

Caine returned fire again as he managed to open the driver's-side door and jump in, but he remained hunched down in the seat while he started up the vehicle. Using the rearview camera, he backed out and away from the storage unit and the gunfire as he tried to call emergency services. Then he shifted into gear to drive away. He ducked just as a bullet hit the windshield. He dropped the phone down by his feet, and it had disconnected with the Bluetooth system so he couldn't complete that call. He had never set the vehicle or his phone to respond to voice commands. Idiot.

"Stay down, Finnley. Please." Desperation edged his demanding tone. He hadn't meant to sound harsh, but he would need to ask for grace on that.

They were in trouble.

Tires squealed, and he rotated the steering wheel left and then right and left again as he sped out of the storage unit parking lot, glad that the woman at the front office was long gone.

He wouldn't want anyone to get hurt. The place had been deserted. Maybe that's part of why the shooters felt emboldened.

"Finnley, are you okay?"

"Yes. It hurts, but I think it's just...just a graze."

"It could have taken muscle. I'll get you to a hospital. I'm so sorry."

He sped away from the Emmons Budget Storage. The town was small, and he remembered where he'd seen a hospital. "Can you use your cell to call the police and tell them what happened?"

"Yes. I'll contact the sheriff's offices." Which she did, but her voice was strained as she told them everything.

"Now call Everly for me and tell her what happened. She was right to warn us to leave."

I shouldn't have gone there.

"We couldn't have known what we would find. It could have been old junk or more stuff for the store for all we knew. Don't blame yourself. If you're going to blame anyone, let it be my father. He could have prepared me for this day. He had to know it was coming."

Caine sped into the small Emmons Regional Hospital, parked close to the ER and rushed Finnley through the emergency department entrance, calling out for help and explaining that she'd been shot. She was rushed away from him, but he refused to leave, explaining that he was her bodyguard hired for protection and she had been shot.

A security guard then appeared, and Caine explained his status and showed his PI license. The security guard allowed him through but confiscated his weapon. He understood—rules were rules—but he explained to the security guard that he should remain vigilant.

Someone could attack them in the hospital.

Inside the small private room, a nurse pulled the curtain so that Finnley could be tended to. He heard some huffs and grunts coming from the other side. "Finnley, what's happening. Are you okay?"

"Yes, Caine. It hurts, that's all. I didn't mean to make so much noise. Please, can you just wait outside the door."

"Okay, fine." He let himself out and stood outside the door. This was better anyway. He didn't think the nurse—a fifty plus stocky woman with a warm and friendly smile—was one of the bad guys. He'd been wrong before, but no. The bad guys hadn't planted a nurse here in the hospital for this moment.

In the meantime, he could talk to his siblings. He called Everly, and she immediately put him on speaker with her, Ayden and Brett.

"Who could have shot at us? Ambushed us at that storage unit?" He tried to keep his voice down. He should have this conversation in private, but he wouldn't leave Finnley, nor would he wait to talk about it. He wanted answers now.

He turned and pressed a fisted hand against the wall, holding back his anger or else he might punch it, which would quickly get him escorted from the hospital.

Ayden spoke over the phone. "I think it's time to bring her into headquarters. We'll keep her safe here."

"I don't know if I can talk her into that."

"Even after getting shot?"

"I don't know, Ayden. So we need a plan B, and on top of that, we need to figure this out."

"Caine, the sheriff's department is going to find you there, and you'll need to hand over the padlock key. They can break off the lock, but they want the key."

"I don't think they need to be the ones to open that unit."

"It goes through them first, and then other agencies will get involved if necessary."

"Other agencies. Who, exactly? ATF?" With all the weapons, he wouldn't doubt the involvement the Bureau of Alcohol, Tobacco, Firearms and Explosives.

"I don't know yet. But you need to keep your eyes on the big picture. She hired you to find out who killed her father because no one was taking her seriously. They are now. She needs to be kept safe, and so you focus on that, okay? The stakes are obviously much higher, and we don't know who we're dealing with," Everly said.

"Scratch that," Ayden said. "We could be dealing with some serious people who know what they're doing."

"Assassins." Caine kept his voice low. "You mean assassins."

"Possibly. Except if it had been true professionals at the unit today or at the apartment the other night, we wouldn't be having a conversation, because you would both be dead. In any case, you're in danger by proximity."

"I've always been in danger by proximity." *Come on, guys. This isn't about me.*

"At some point, if they continue to try to come at Finnley, these people will take you out to get to her. I want you to bring her in."

"Even if she agrees to that, I'm not sure I can convince her to close the shop. She… She doesn't think like that. Work like that. I know she's having misgivings about who her father was, but she's not the kind of person to give up. Not on her father. Not on her work. Working at that shop, living above it, is the only life she's known."

Even if it was a life built on lies. The Wilbanks & Co. shop was a front for something. Until Caine learned who was behind the attacks, the danger to Finnley would only grow. Caine closed his eyes, nausea rising in his stomach.

How do I protect you, Finnley?

An old movie—*North by Northwest* with Gregory Peck, if she remembered correctly—played on the big widescreen secured to the wall.

Finnley was too stunned to fight back, to argue with Caine. Much.

She'd taken some painkillers too, and because she trusted him implicitly—probably a bad idea—she found herself sitting in a comfortable living space in a home theater connected to their headquarters. It was considered safe because of all the precautionary measures in place. Though the location had long ago been compromised, the address wasn't public or easily acquired.

Finnley was surprised she remembered that much. She lolled her head back against the sofa and closed her eyes.

I shouldn't have taken the painkillers.

At least they were wearing off now, and she much preferred the slight pain in her upper arm to the lack of control or decision-making abilities.

"Why are we here?" She rolled her head to Caine.

He slouched on the sofa too, looking both pained and relaxed. She lifted her hand and touched his cheek. "You're so cute."

"And you're a little drugged." He chuckled. "And cute too."

A throat cleared, and Caine sat up tall and glanced over his shoulder.

"Maybe she should rest." The woman came all the way into the room. Everly Honor.

"I remember you." Finnley smiled. "I saw you in your office working on your computers when I first came to HPS to meet with Ayden."

Everly's smile was warm and friendly. "I'll help you get to your room and into bed so you can sleep the pain meds off."

"No. I don't want to sleep. I want to talk. I'm good. They're wearing off." She refused to move even when Everly tried to assist her to her feet.

"I have to get to work," Finnley said.

"It's too late," Caine said. "After hours. You need to recover, Finnley."

"Caine, you promised. You assured me that I could still go into my shop for a few hours every day."

He pursed his lips and focused on her face, then his gaze shifted to her eyes. "I didn't promise. Nothing is set in stone. We have to keep adjusting as needed. Don't you remember? You were shot."

The words sent a pang through her. "I won't stay here."

"No one is forcing you. You're here for your safety. We'll talk about that later."

When you can be reasonable. He didn't say it, but she saw that look on both their faces. And they were right. She wasn't feeling like herself. But something nagged at the back of her mind. Maybe it had been there all along, but she had been so tense, so scared that she hadn't paid attention. Now, sitting here so relaxed she thought about what was bugging her.

"I feel like I need to be there so someone can contact me."

"What?" both siblings said simultaneously.

Caine shifted closer. "What are you talking about? What do you mean?"

"I'm saying that someone out there knows what's going on. If I disappear, we won't ever find out. I need to be at the store. You can be there too, Caine, and protect me."

He looked up at Everly, who crossed her arms.

"You think I'm being unreasonable."

"That's not it," Everly said. "I think you're being brave by putting yourself out there, but solving this case is not worth risking your life."

"You, Everly or Ayden or Brett can take up space in the apartment across the street. Nobody's going to get to me or hurt me. You'll be there." She turned to Caine. "And tomorrow, you can teach me how to shoot."

And with that, Finnley stood. Dizziness almost sent her into Caine's arms, but he moved quickly and stood, steadying her.

"I'll walk her to her room, Everly."

She didn't want him to think she was an invalid, but she liked his nearness. She sensed that Everly walked behind them, not giving them privacy. Not trusting her own brother?

Maybe she saw there was something between Finnley and Caine, because there was, wasn't there? Even though she didn't want there to be. Letting herself fall for this guy would only lead to heartache, and she'd already suffered enough.

At her room, Caine opened the door and Everly started inside.

"No," Finnley said. "I'd like some privacy with Caine."

"I...don't think that's a good idea. Our policy is that I help you."

"Caine has been living in my apartment." Finnley wasn't sure where that had come from. At the very least, she hated people trying to control her. "I can handle myself."

Caine sent his sister an apologetic look and entered the room with Finnley. He took a seat in the chair by the desk and almost acted as if he was afraid of her.

"What gives, Finnley?"

"What gives?"

She sensed that whatever was between them before in the small apartment and all their cloak-and-dagger had shifted.

Squeezing her eyes shut, she fisted her hands and tried to control her shaking. "Caine, I..."

Suddenly, she was in his arms. He'd rushed to her and held her. Not because she was scared... No, this was more than that. She *hadn't* imagined what was happening between them.

"Caine," she said again. "This can't happen."

"I know, Finnley." He eased back enough to look at her, his face, his lips mere millimeters away. "I know it can't. I told you a little about Sophie before. Well, she died in my arms, and I don't know if I'll ever get over that. I just know that I don't want to hurt you. I shouldn't be here in your room holding you like this."

She stepped out of his arms. "I guess we're just two broken people then. I had two bad breakups, and I don't trust myself to know when it's okay." She wasn't making any sense. Why was she even telling him?

"What happened?" He tucked a loose strand of her hair behind her ear. She was so sweet and tender and making it even harder for him to resist her.

"In high school, my 'boyfriend' tried to take advantage of me. When I refused, he dumped me. He was a football player, and I was a bookish nerd. I should have known that he didn't really care about me. Then in college, I took a chance, a risk, and I let myself fall again. I should have known that Ezra wasn't someone I could trust. We dated and grew serious, or so I thought." A knot lodged in her throat. "I thought he was going to propose, but my best friend told me that he was cheating on me with other women. I don't know if he ever would have proposed because I confronted him, and we broke up. I was crushed."

Finnley hated how vulnerable she felt sharing with him, and anguish coursed through her.

"You don't have to worry about me." He gently pressed his lips to her forehead. "Sleep well, Finnley. I'm here for you as long as you need. Um…outside your room. I'll be right across the hall."

He released her, slowly walked to the door and then turned to smile at her over his shoulder. A sad smile, though. Not one of pity, but she understood. They were both much too damaged. Neither of them could risk more together.

Finnley thought she was strong, but she had a feeling that she was weak when it came to resisting Caine Honor.

A soft knock came at the door, and Everly peeked in. "I

don't mean to keep you. I want to make sure you have everything you need. I hung up a few of your clothes in the closet. There's a private bathroom with all the toiletries, including a few of yours." She clasped her hands as if waiting on Finnley.

"Thank you."

Another step forward. "My brother is the best and will protect you with his life."

"I know." What was Everly getting at?

"I'm not sure he is the best bet in matters of the heart. I owe you both that much. That warning. Take care, Finnley."

Then Everly walked out.

Finnley didn't appreciate the interference in something so personal.

Still, I can't get close to him. I swore off love. It causes too much pain. She was in the middle of trying to solve her father's murder. *What's the matter with me?*

Caine.

Caine was the matter with her.

TWELVE

At the shooting range just outside town, Caine wrapped his arms around Finnley to show her how to hold the gun and how to aim. He hadn't thought he'd need to get so close.

Arms around her snugly, being careful to avoid her injury, he positioned the gun just so. Then he placed his head against hers, his cheek next her ear. He feared she might hear his heart pounding. Or see his hands shaking.

Caine, get a grip.

Maybe he needed to step away from this assignment, for both their sakes. But the stakes had never been higher for him. He wouldn't let anyone else get close to Finnley to harm her.

Or protect her. No one was as determined as he was to keep her safe.

To find Frank's killer.

So close to her now, he could smell the mixture of citrus and vanilla. He tried to focus. To concentrate.

She'd wanted him to show her how to hold a gun and gestured for him to show her in this manner. He stepped away, hoping to break the crazy rush of emotion.

He lowered the gun she aimed at the target and took it from her. "Before you actually shoot, we need to put these on." He handed her the earmuffs. "This will protect your hearing and mine."

They each put on earmuffs.

"Are you ready?" he asked.

Her smile was timid, but beautiful. "Yes. I need to do this."

"Okay. Do as I showed you." He handed the gun over.

She lifted it toward the target.

"Wait. First, chamber a round."

"Oh, right."

"Look down the barrel just like we talked about. Finger on the trigger."

"I'm going to need you to stop talking so I can concentrate."

He stifled a laugh at that and kept his mouth shut. He didn't say another word. Instead, he stood back and watched Finnley. She seemed like such a gentle creature, and he wanted to protect her at all costs, but he'd seen how strong she was in the face of the worst kind of nightmare. She was courageous. In case Caine or anyone else failed to protect her, Finnley had the right to protect herself, and this was a first step. Still, it grieved him that her life had come to this. This beautiful, gentle creature, who wasn't accustomed to being around guns, was now forced to both hire protection and learn to use violence to protect herself. Or at least train in how to use a gun and make sure her aim was true.

The other night, he wasn't exactly sure she could have hit the mark when she'd aimed at the intruder in the apartment.

She fired multiple shots, emptying the cartridge. Only one even came close to hitting the center of the paper target. Finnley lowered the gun and frowned.

Her lips puckered into a pout. "This is harder than it looks. I hope you're not disappointed."

"Why would I be disappointed? It takes practice. That's what a shooting range is for. Experienced and seasoned professionals and enthusiasts come here regularly to train. To practice. You can't expect to hit the bull's-eye or get a head shot or chest shot first try. But this time, just go for center mass."

"Huh?"

"The biggest part of the target. The torso, the chest. Not to get too graphic, but you're aiming at the heart and lungs."

Her face twisted up in a big cringe. "Why can't I shoot them in the leg? I don't really want to kill anyone."

How did he explain without getting too graphic. "Center mass is the largest target, and you have more chance of hitting the largest target. In the moments when you're in self-defense mode, it all happens fast. For the average person, responding to deadly force is stressful, and fear can shut you down. But aiming at the largest target—again, center mass or the chest just below the neck—is your best chance of success during an intense situation. Any questions?"

She squeezed her eyes shut, scrunched her nose, then opened her eyes and stared at him. "You mentioned bull's-eye. Do you happen to have one of those kinds of targets? I'd rather practice shooting at a sheet of paper with all the circles and aim at the center."

He drew in a long breath and released it. "If you aren't able to shoot a person to defend yourself, there's no point to this exercise." Now he sounded harsh, like his dad who'd taken them out and taught them how to use a rifle to hunt when they were kids. If they weren't able to shoot to kill, they had no business having a gun. Someone could just take it from them and use it against them. That was exactly his concern with Finnley.

"Finnley, I'm sorry. It's just…"

"No, I get it. I understand. Don't be easy on me. I appreciate that you're trying to help me learn how to use a gun. If I can't use it, then it's dangerous to me."

"Yes. That's it."

"Let's keep practicing then. Give me some time to wrap my mind around it."

He nodded and gave her a few more pointers, then they spent another hour target shooting. He practiced too. After several rounds of ammo—this wasn't an inexpensive endeavor—

Finnley was finally getting the hang of it and was able to shoot and hit center mass repeatedly.

When she turned and gave him her beautiful smile, he knew he was in trouble. She laughed. And then she suddenly went serious. The smile fled. She stayed close to him, connected. He closed his eyes, savoring the nearness but fighting the need to kiss her.

Seriously?

They were at a shooting range. If anyone stopped shooting at targets, they might notice the two ridiculous shooters. He leaned toward her, drawn by her beauty and strength. She'd shown such determination during their training. "You did well, Finnley."

Then he stepped away. What had just happened? He let his heart rate slow and took a few calming breaths.

Why ask the question when he knew the answer? He was getting entirely too close to her. Worse, he didn't care.

He'd never thought he could love anyone after Sophie. Or rather, he'd refused to love anyone after Sophie. His heart couldn't take the pain of loss again.

Finnley was nothing like Sophie, but she'd still found her way into his heart and brought him back to life. He had to find a way to escape her before it was too late. And the only way to do that was to solve this.

"I think we're done." The words came out a little too brusque, and seeing the hurt in her eyes hurt him too. He smiled to smooth off the edges. "I'll take those earmuffs from you, that is, if you're ready to give them up."

Warmth flashed in her eyes again, but it was diminished from moments before. He'd done that to her. To them both by severing the connection. Just as well.

Finnley practically fell into the seat of Caine's muscle car, a red Dodge Charger—the Ford Escape was out of commission as it looked like it'd been used for target practice. She was grateful for the reprieve. At first, she'd been energized after finally making the center-mass shot multiple times. That had given her a bit of confidence, but in truth, she hoped to never have to be forced to pull the trigger. It apparently took ten days for a background check before her purchase would be released to her. If she picked it up today, she wasn't sure her hands could even hold it. They were so tired after repeatedly firing that handgun. She might even have a few blisters and frankly, her shoulder was throbbing a little.

He steered them away from Rainier Indoor Tactical, and she thought back to those last moments when she'd found success. Jumping for joy inside, she'd practically jumped into Caine's arms. She might have imagined it, but it had sure felt like he was going to kiss her. And she'd wanted that kiss. Sharing her excitement with him had given her a sense of accomplishment, and it had felt good to have someone to share it with. Someone she cared about.

But just like that, his attitude had shifted when he stepped away from her. Between the two of them, he was the smart one.

She settled into the seat and noticed how he took the curvy roads a little too fast for her comfort, seeming to enjoy driving his fast car. "We're going to the shop, now, right? That was the plan."

"Yes. We're sticking to the plan. You can work a few hours, and be sure to put up a new sign for reduced days and hours so your customers will know. Have you decided what those will be yet?"

"I'm still thinking on it. While you drive, I'll just close my eyes and rest for a few minutes." She bit her lip, wishing she hadn't added those words. Lately, it seemed like she didn't have much stamina, but she would give herself a break. She was under a lot of strain.

"I think that's a good idea, but you don't have to go to work.

I can take you back to headquarters, and you can rest there and go in tomorrow instead."

"The shop is all I have left of Dad. All I have left, period." She hadn't really thought about it before she'd said the words.

Caine said nothing more.

What was there to say? She closed her eyes and tried to relax for a few minutes. The drive back to Emmons would take forty-five minutes at least. But she couldn't get Caine out of her heart and mind.

The way he'd wrapped his arms around her to show her how to use the gun. He hadn't really needed to do that, but she'd asked him to. She had no clue why. But he had, and she'd savored the feel of his arms around her, the feel of his strong biceps, the smell of him. No question, she was attracted to this guy.

She must be losing it, really losing it.

But that wasn't all. He'd been so gentle and caring and compassionate through this entire ordeal. He'd broken through the barriers of her heart.

What am I going to do? She'd been a terrible judge of character when it came to trusting men with her heart.

Just last night, she'd sworn off Caine.

Even if she hadn't, this was still the wrong time. Dad had been murdered.

Still, Caine was making her wonder if she could stick to her resolve. After this was over, Caine would go back to his job, and she'd have to find her way in this world without her father.

Without Caine.

"Finnley. Finnley..." A soft nudge against her arm startled her, then she realized Caine had said her name a few times.

She rubbed her eyes. "I can't believe I actually fell asleep."

She glanced at him and found him close. Maybe too close, but they were doing that a lot lately, and she could not move.

He studied her. "Are you sure you want to work this afternoon?"

"Yes. I need this."

"Okay. I parked up a few blocks and watched the place. Drove around back. Saw no one, though I've yet to see our stalkers watching the place during the day. I need to clear it first. The cameras are up and running, but they could have been hacked. We could walk into a surprise. You ready?"

"As I'll ever be."

"Then let's go."

She stepped out in front of Emmons New York Bagels. "We're three blocks away."

"Yep."

"I could use the fresh air and walk anyway."

"We both could. Anyone watching the shop won't see what vehicle we exited. I'll have to change out the Dodge, though."

"Yeah, not real subtle, Caine." She sent him a teasing smile.

"I needed to take her out. She gets twitchy when I don't. She needs the exercise."

"You're funny." *Did people really think like that about their cars?* She hadn't owned a car she cared that much about.

"Apparently." He grabbed her hand as they walked along the sidewalk together as a couple.

Which they weren't.

"If you weren't sticking so close to me, you'd be out driving your car you clearly love every day."

"I work protective details a lot. I was only kidding about the car. That's just horse talk from my past. Dad would tell us to take the horse for a ride because it needed exercise."

She paused and tugged him back to her. "How much longer is this going to take?"

"Finnley, we'll find something, a clue, something, and get to the truth soon. Plus, the sheriff's department is working on this."

"And other agencies are getting involved now after the storage unit discovery?"

His expression was solemn, and his hazel eyes serious, filled with regret. "Yes."

She started walking again, though she had a feeling Caine had more to say. Was he going to quit on her before they found answers? After all, with law enforcement actually involved, what did she need Caine for? Well, except for protection. The attacks on her had ramped up. Was he trying to find out if she wanted him to continue?

Yes, she did. Very much. But maybe not completely one hundred percent for the right reasons. She unlocked the front door to the shop and opened the blinds. Caine cleared the downstairs, and she followed him upstairs to her apartment that had been released as a crime scene.

"Caine?"

"Yeah?" He put his gun into the holster.

"Are we staying here or across the street tonight?"

"We're staying at the headquarters, remember? It's too dangerous to stay in town. During the day, work a few hours. It'll be safe."

She went down the steps and back into the shop and opened up the register.

"What's really bothering you?" Caine paced around the small space of the store.

Everything. Nothing. I don't know.

Maybe she was wrong. Maybe this wasn't all she had. The shop, this life, couldn't be everything to her because...because she didn't know if she could live here anymore. Do this anymore.

THIRTEEN

I don't like this.

It wasn't the first time Caine had protected someone in danger who insisted on continuing with their life. Protecting someone in danger while they continued their day-to-day life was merely one aspect of PPD—personal protection detail.

Sometimes clients were too hardheaded for their own good. Finnley's case was a tough one because yes, she was stubborn about keeping her father's business—*her* business now—going, but also because the shop was all she had left of her father—the only family in her life.

Caine didn't have the heart to force the issue. Hers wasn't the first detail like this he'd worked.

With his siblings' help, they'd put as many safety measures in place as they could in these circumstances. The cameras were working, and the town was alive, bustling with the usual tempo. Nothing felt off to him.

The fall day was sunny and bright. Unfortunately, that meant a person could easily sink into complacency or feel like all was well. Caine wouldn't be fooled by any of it. The danger remained.

Finnley had perked up when a couple of customers had come in. He'd seen them before around town, and Finnley seemed to know them well. Still, Caine scrutinized each person who entered, even if they were locals and she knew them well. Often deadly deeds were committed by familiar parties. People were killed or preyed on by those they already knew and believed trustworthy. It's what allowed them to get close enough to commit murder. Or at times someone close to a target was blackmailed or coerced into committing a heinous crime by another party.

Yeah, he didn't like this one bit and wouldn't let his guard down.

Caine had seen it all.

His cell rang, and he answered it only because Everly might have something important for him. But he continued to watch Finnley and her customers closely. Unfortunately, he had to work hard to push thoughts of this morning out of his mind when he'd been so close to Finnley that he could smell her shampoo.

She'd focused and worked hard until she'd accomplished her task to aim and shoot a gun when she'd never held one before. Her father had lied to her, claiming he hated guns, and yet he'd kept a stash in a storage unit. Finnley must be hurting, and yet she pushed past the pain and kept going. He admired her courage and strength. Her heart.

"Caine, are you listening?"

"Yep. Well. Nope. Tell me again."

Everly harrumphed her disapproval. *Please, don't give me a lecture.*

"What's up?" he asked.

"How's she doing?"

"She's in her element. I think she needs this, honestly," he said. "But I'm going to push to get her out of this situation for the time being."

"I agree."

You do? "Why did you really call?"

"Right. Well, I've been digging deep, like we discussed, on Finnley's father."

"And?"

"We already know that he isn't who he claimed to be and was possibly in hiding. If he'd been a witness in hiding through WITSEC, I think I would have learned that by now through the U.S. Marshals. I'm leaning more toward him being part of a government agency, but I can't confirm that either. I just want you to be extra careful."

"You know I am. Any news on who might have been driving the Tahoe?"

"Detective Mann let me know that the owner's sister had cameras. I don't know why she didn't notice the vehicle was stolen, but she was on vacation in Hawaii, so maybe that's answer enough. So they have footage and are trying to identify the thief. He was dressed in all black with a hood and took the vehicle in the night."

"So it's not likely you'll identify him."

"With the technology we have today, there's a small chance that his gait will be recognized or his facial features, even with the mask. But the good news is that the vehicle was found, and they're trying to pull DNA. The person behind this is a professional, but even they make mistakes."

"And mistakes are how criminals—no matter their skills and experience or mastermind level—are caught."

"Masterminds are human."

"But this isn't about a mastermind or one person, is it?"

"I believe the men who have followed and attacked Finnley, who killed her father, are working for someone. His death was a hit, I believe. Finnley would have been killed too had she not gone out for those few minutes."

"I wish you could figure out why Frank—an antique stationery store owner—was hiding his true identity. Why this store?"

"And that's why I called. While you're there, please look closely at everything. I can't help but think he chose that option for a reason. There has to be something about the store that will give us a clue about him, and maybe lead us to who he really is."

"That's a stretch, don't you think?" Caine watched a customer leave, and relief filled him. Maybe the store would be empty for a few minutes, and he would ask Finnley about cutting her hours short today and getting out of here.

"Right now, every little detail matters. Nothing is a stretch in this situation."

"I got you."

A nicely dressed woman wearing a wide-brimmed fedora that half covered her face entered the store. Finnley brightened up when she saw the woman.

"Is Frank in?" the woman asked.

Finnley visibly paled, and her mouth dropped open as her hand covered her chest and slid to her throat.

"I gotta go," Caine said to his sister.

Only one customer had asked for Dad since his death, but Finnley hadn't known the customer who had ordered customized stationery over the phone. No frequent customers had asked for Dad. Not since his death. How could Mrs. Tomlinson not know?

Then again, why would she know? She didn't actually live in town and drove all the way from Seattle. The slender woman in her sixties claimed she adored this shop and everything about it, and that's why she visited often. Each time, she would talk to Dad.

Maybe that explained Finnley's reaction to her question. "I'm… I'm sorry. My father isn't here. He… He passed on."

Finnley blinked back tears. Pursing her lips, she thought through what she might say next. Did Mrs. Tomlinson need to know the details? Probably not.

The woman appeared shaken—shocked, even. Her eyes

shimmered as she glanced around the shop. Her mouth opened, but she said nothing as she reached for Finnley and then snatched her hand back. "I'm sorry. I have to go."

Mrs. Tomlinson abruptly turned and rushed out of the store, the bell over the door ringing violently in her wake. Finnley stared after her, feeling the surprise of the moment rushing all around her. At the same time, it left her numb.

Caine locked the door and turned the Closed sign over.

"What are you doing?"

"It's time to close." He approached the counter. "Are you okay?"

"I don't know." Finnley began closing out the register. "I wasn't expecting that question. It hit me wrong today."

"You know that woman?"

"Mrs. Tomlinson comes in every couple of months. I don't know why I expected her to know that my father is gone. Not *everyone* knows he's gone. She doesn't live in town, so it's not like she would read the obituaries or see the news here."

Caine's intense interest in Mrs. Tomlinson scared Finnley.

"She asked if Frank was in. Does she normally talk to your father?" he asked.

"If he was here, they would step outside and chat."

"About what, exactly?"

Finnley looked up from counting bills. "How would I know? They were always outside when they talked. I could see them through the window, but Dad talked to a lot of customers. She's just one of them. Why does it matter? Why all the questions?"

"I'm just curious if she's someone who has known your father for a long time."

"Lots of people have known him a long time." Finnley tried to focus on closing the register, but her energy was almost depleted. "None of them knew his real identity, though."

"That we know of. Maybe that's what we need to do next.

Look into all his customers and see if there's a connection to his old identity there."

She finished counting and had to recount, then she finished up closing out the register and locked the money in the small safe in her dad's office until it could be deposited. She plopped into the chair at his desk.

Caine was taking special interest in the stacks of vintage-looking stationery today. More than usual. But Finnley didn't care. Maybe she should.

"Are we going to stay across the street tonight?" She stood and pushed the chair under the desk.

"What? You know where we're staying." He studied her as if concerned.

"Oh, that's right. I'm tired." And shaken after the encounter with the longtime customer she barely knew.

"You sure you're okay?"

"Come on, Caine. It's been a long day. Can we just go now?"

"Yes." He offered a sympathetic smile. "You're right, it *has* been a long day, and you accomplished a lot."

She appreciated his understanding and the compliment. "Let me get my purse. Are we leaving the lights on upstairs?"

"I have timers on the television and the lights. They come on and go off."

Why did she keep forgetting all this? Still… "Do you really think we're fooling anyone?"

He lifted a shoulder. "It's better than leaving the place looking empty. Signs of life are a good thing."

"Even if those signs of life draw the attention of the wrong people?"

"If I spot the watcher back here—via the cameras—I'll contact the local sheriff's department. Let Everly know. Maybe whatever agency she claims is interested will take him down."

"And we'll find out once and for all who killed my father and maybe who he really was." Though honestly, she doubted that would happen. He had a secret life for a reason. "I just hope he wasn't some sort of gangster or bad guy."

"Oh, Finnley. You can't believe that. No matter what your father did in the past or what secretive job he had, he was still the same man you knew and loved, at least the part that matters was."

I wish I could believe that. I just don't know.

Someone banged on the glass door, startling her.

Caine pushed her behind him and pulled his gun.

"Oh, Caine, it's just Mrs. Tomlinson. You're scaring her. Put your gun away."

"Stay here." Caine approached the door and spoke to her through the glass. "We're closed now."

She knocked frantically. "Please, hurry, let me in. I need to talk to you," she said, her voice muted by the glass.

Finnley rushed around him and unlocked the door. "She's a customer. Let her in."

Distraught, the woman stepped inside and looked around before her gaze landed on Finnley. She leaned in and whispered, "You're in danger."

Then she stuck a slip of paper in Finnley's hand and dashed out the door, leaving Finnley to stare after her.

What was that about? Finnley started after her, opening the door. "Wait!"

Bullets pelted the glass, drowning out her voice.

FOURTEEN

"Down. Get down!" Caine dived for Finnley, shoving her to the ground. Covering her. Protecting her. They'd hit the ground pretty hard.

Fear for her gripped him, but he focused on doing his job. Another round of gunfire shattered the shop's glass door.

Finnley screamed under him, and he covered her as glass showered them. She'd been so close to the door when the gunfire erupted. And what of Mrs. Tomlinson? Had an innocent bystander gotten caught in the cross fire or something more? Had she gotten away, or was she collapsed on the sidewalk?

Given the odd communication, she had to be involved somehow. Surely someone in town had called the police if they weren't already arriving on the scene. All these thoughts swirled through his mind while he concentrated on how to keep her safe and what was happening around them. Situational awareness.

Heart hammering, he caught his breath and moved away enough to look at her. He feared Finnley had been shot.

"Are you okay?" he asked. "You're not shot, are you?"

"No. I'm okay. Just a little bruised maybe." She was breathing erratically. "But you saved me. I'm good with that."

"I didn't mean to hurt you."

"Can we get out of here?"

"Yes." Another bullet hit the shop. "Let's go behind the counter."

Crouching, they maneuvered over behind the protection of the counter made of heavy, hard wood. They both gasped for breath. Heart pounding, he tried to figure out how best to protect her. With his cell, he looked at the cameras, but whoever had shot at them was well hidden and out of the camera's view.

"My dad's shop. Look at the windows. They'll have to be replaced." Finnley said the words between heavy breaths.

She'd been shot at, and her concern was for her father's shop. He wouldn't say it, but he suspected her father would care more about her life than his shop. The question that followed was why was he involved in something so clandestine that it had brought this danger to her door?

The woman—Mrs. Tomlinson—had distracted him. That entire exchange had been weird. She'd had a sense of urgency. Had she known about the coming barrage of gunfire, and if so, maybe she should have been more direct?

"What about Mrs. Tomlinson, Caine? Do you think she got shot? We need to check on her." She started to crawl forward, and bullets slammed into the wooden counter, thankfully not penetrating.

"Are you out of your mind? No. We can't check on her. I'm sure the county sheriff's department is on their way from some far reach of the county, but I'm going to call anyway. One of them or emergency services can check on her if she was shot. She could have gotten clear, though, before the shooting started. We just don't know."

Using his cell, he called 911 and informed them of the situation. Dispatch told him that deputies were on the way. Caine explained to the dispatcher that he was in protection mode, and he could not stay on the line, then he ended the call.

"Help will be here soon," he said. "But we can't wait here

for them." Whoever was shooting was going to come right through that door for her.

"Where are we going?" Her voice shook.

"Out the back." If that option was available.

He wanted to cover her and lay down gunfire, but he could accidentally hit an innocent bystander. He hoped that everyone downtown had the good sense to get far away from this scene, but Caine couldn't shoot without an actual target.

A quick assessment of the angle of gunfire led him to believe that initially it had come from the apartment over Ye Olde Antique Shop across the street. Now it appeared to come from directly across the street.

"Try to stay behind the displays and behind me. Let's go!"

They went around the counter and toward the back of the shop. More bullets rained through the window, hitting stationery and papers and old books. Paper bits exploded in the air like confetti with each shot.

In the back hallway, he wanted to catch his breath, but there wasn't time. They had been herded to the back. He glanced at his watch and saw on the camera that an unfriendly was breaking into the back.

"What's going on?" Finnley was hyperventilating between her questions. "Aren't we going to get out of here?"

"Can't." He aimed his gun at the door and walked backward. "Quick. Up the stairs."

She ran upstairs, and he raced after her. Caine locked the upstairs door. "Let's hope the deputies get here in time to stop this before it goes too far."

"It's a big county. Since we're stuck in here, it looks like we'll have to wait for help to arrive, after all." She turned in circles. "What are we going to do, Caine? Are we going to die?"

"No. Don't think like that." He tugged the Glock 42 subcompact .380 from his ankle holster and pressed it in her hand.

"But I'm still waiting on my background check. I can't—"

"Desperate times, Finnley. You know how to shoot. You know how to defend yourself."

He looked at the camera footage on his watch. They'd been shot out. *Great.* He stared out the windows both front and back. Whoever was coming in the back was probably already at the apartment door.

"Go to the bedroom. Hide in the closet and shoot anyone who opens the door."

"Except you."

"Except me or a deputy. Use your judgment."

Fear emanated from her, then she chambered a round in the gun and nodded. Confident. Good. She was more resilient than he'd imagined she could be. Probably even more than she'd imagined.

"Desperate times." She took off and then returned.

"What?"

She marched forward, tugged his collar forward and planted a kiss on his lips. Then she stood back. "Be careful."

"I will. Please…go…" He wished she hadn't done that, because he needed to focus. She must have kissed him in case she never got the chance after tonight.

She raced down the short hallway and into her room. He heard the door shut.

He aimed at the door to the apartment. He couldn't let anyone in. But…they should have burst through the door by now. What was going on?

Then he knew… He realized the tactic before the evidence hit his nostrils.

Smoke billowed up from beneath the door. *No!* Caine rushed forward and touched the knob. Hot. It was already hot. Someone must have deliberately started a fire in the stairwell. He smelled the gasoline now too—an accelerant to make sure it burned fast and hot.

They'd been driven upstairs to trap them. Upstairs to die.

* * *

Finnley hadn't wanted to leave Caine to battle alone, but by now, she understood him well enough to know that he would focus better on taking the bad guys out if she wasn't there to distract him. She would give him all the help he needed by staying hidden and safe.

And she could pray.

Finnley opened the closet door and shoved the shoes over. She slid down to the floor behind the hanging clothes and prepared herself emotionally and mentally to do what needed to be done. Maybe they should have used her father's secret office as a safe room for hiding instead. But it was always easier think about what you should have done in hindsight. Now she was at the bottom of the closet, aiming the small pistol at the door.

Lord, please don't let me shoot someone who doesn't need to be shot.

Her body trembled as tears and emotion built up in her throat. Now wasn't the time to pour out everything she'd kept inside for so long. She wiped at the tears. How was she going to protect herself like this? She had to be strong.

Lord, I need answers. I need to know who my father really was. Who killed him. I need to know who I really am.

Scripture rushed at her. Ephesians 2:10. *"For we are his workmanship, created in Christ Jesus unto good works, which God hath before ordained that we should walk in them."*

What good work is it You want me to do, God?

Finnley shook off the thoughts. Now wasn't the time.

Why hadn't she heard gunfire? Why hadn't Caine come in to tell her that it was over?

She sniffed. Was that…?

"Smoke," she whispered. *Oh. No.*

She quickly stood and stared at the door in the dark closet. What should she do? Caine told her to stay hidden until he came to get her, or someone in law enforcement came for her. But staying here to burn alive wasn't an option. Caine must be hurt. Or worse. No, she wouldn't let her mind go there.

What do I do? What do I do?

"Finnley!" he shouted. "Finnley, where are you?"

She opened the door. "In the closet like you told me. I smell smoke."

"They trapped us and set the place on fire."

"Did you call for help again?"

"Yes, and I told them about the fire. But we could die before they get here."

"Wait. I hear a siren or two. The volunteer fire department is coming!" Finnley coughed, the acrid smoke already getting to her. "With the kind of items in the store, this place is going to go up way too fast."

"Right. And any other evidence left by your father that we might have found in the store is going up in flames," he said.

"Maybe that's why they're doing it. They killed Dad, tried to kill me or get at me, but that didn't work. Maybe they know they couldn't find what they need in this massive shop, so now they're going to take us out with it."

While she talked, Caine worked. He wet towels and stuffed them under the door. The smoke might not get to them yet, but the flames were coming. Already, paint bubbled on the walls from the heat.

Sweat beaded her brow, and her heart pounded erratically. *Oh, Dad...*

What could have been so important that they killed her father and now wanted to kill her too?

Caine gripped her arms. "We can't wait on the firefighters."

"No, we can't. We could go out the window. There are still fire escape stairs on these old buildings."

"They expect us to go out that way and will shoot to keep us inside."

He ran to the window and glanced out. A bullet hit the glass, and he pressed against the wall. Caine held her gaze, fear in his eyes. Fear and fury and deep grief.

She'd never seen that look before. Even Caine was scared. Nothing had ever terrified her more.

"Caine?" Her voice sounded shaky. "I have an idea."

FIFTEEN

As Caine listened to her suggestion, he wasn't so sure about it.

"A door to another hidden room? Your father had a thing about hidden rooms. But another room isn't going to free us from this situation."

"You don't understand. I'm talking about a door to the roof. This is an old building, and this space was renovated for the apartment. When I was a kid, I took the small flight of steps up to the roof. Dad was concerned for my safety and didn't want me playing on the roof, so he blocked it with a bookshelf, which makes sense, but he left the door—another escape if needed?" She shrugged. "Over time, I forgot it was even there. Until now."

It was worth a try. Anything was worth a try if it meant saving their lives. He never should have let this situation spiral into this predicament, but he could review and debrief after they survived.

"This shelf. It has to be behind this shelf. Help me," she said. "We need to move it. We can't waste time like you did in Dad's secret office and remove the books. We should just push it over."

"No, wait. Do you remember if the door opens out or in?"

"I don't know." She shrugged and chewed her lip.

"Then we need to completely move the shelf out of the way. Pushing it over could mean blocking the door." Together, they begin moving enough books so the shelf wouldn't be so heavy.

"I guess Dad thought he might one day need an escape."

"I'm glad, because this is giving us hope. And once we're up there, we can cross over to other buildings. I don't think they'll see or can shoot at us there. They'd need to be at the right angle to take the shot," Caine said.

It all depended on how determined and prepared they were. They could certainly be in position somewhere, but this was Caine and Finnley's only choice.

Once most of the books had been tossed across the room, Caine turned to her. "You ready? Let's move this."

They heaved and lifted the old antique bookshelf until it was well out of the way, then it fell onto Finnley's bed, which was crushed under the weight.

Caine was starting to get dizzy with the effort as he sucked in too much smoke.

God, please help us get to safety! Please, save Finnley. Get her out of this. Forgive me for my mistakes and help me make the right decisions.

He moved to open the old door, but it wouldn't budge. *Great.* "Was it sealed shut?"

"I… I don't know." Her hair was already dripping with sweat from the heat of the fire that would soon overtake them.

"I'll help you." Together, they pulled on the old handle.

It broke, and they both fell back into the pile of books.

This couldn't be happening. There was no time to sit and think to figure this out. The building would soon be completely engulfed in flames. The other businesses close by were also in trouble. The whole town had to be out and watching by now.

He peered out the window and spotted a small firetruck—not the big kind one saw in cities. But at least they had arrived. Still, with all the chaos, noise and flames, Caine didn't trust he and Finnley could climb out the windows and take the fire escape without being shot at and forced back inside. Besides, the place was already too engulfed in flames.

"We have to get up on that roof and to another building, Finnley." Before the floor collapsed beneath them. "Stand back."

Caine fired his weapon at what remained of the door handle, opening a hole. He wrapped a thin blanket around his hand so it wouldn't get cut and stuck his hand through and disengaged the lock. The door released. The hinges were rusty and didn't want to move, but he tugged the door fully open, scratching the wood floor along the way. No matter. The floor, all of it, would soon turn to ash.

Better the floor than Caine and Finnley.

"Come on, let's go." He urged her forward and up the steps.

They clanked up the iron stairwell and onto the roof. Around them, the sky was filled with smoke. That was good and bad. For the moment, they were invisible to any hidden shooters that had made a clumsy attempt to kill them in the fire. Caine and Finnley both covered their mouths and noses and headed to the edge of the building that was closest to the next structure. Unfortunately, that building was burning too.

"We have to jump to the next one and keep going until we get free." And just pray they didn't fall and nothing collapsed under them.

She nodded.

"You go first."

"Let's jump together, Caine."

Together, they jumped. She rolled like she was a natural, but Caine landed wrong, and pain spiked up his leg. He stood anyway and grabbed her hand. "Let's keep moving. We don't stop until we're completely safe."

He had no idea when true safety for Finnley would happen, but just getting away from the fire and the shooters would be good enough for the moment. At the end of the neighboring burning building, they hopped across to the next structure. They couldn't go any farther unless they could jump across the alley space there.

"I don't think I can make that," she said.

With his leg injury, he probably couldn't either. Water sprayed on them from another firetruck.

"They must be dousing the neighboring buildings down to protect them if possible."

He crouched and peered off the edge to the fire escape. They'd have to drop down, which would make noise and potentially draw unwanted attention.

"Caine, let's just go down the stairs. Shoot the door open. We can hope the space hasn't been renovated, taking out access to the roof. We'll just go down the steps and out through the store front before it's too late."

"Great idea." He pulled on the door, but it was locked, of course. He shot out the lock again, possibly drawing attention to their plan. He opened the door, and they raced down the stairwell to another locked door. "Don't worry. I'll explain to the owners and the sheriff's offices that we were trying to survive."

"I'm not worried. I trust you to get us out of here."

They raced through storage room and down to the first floor of the local pharmacy. The pharmacy staff hovered on the sidewalk in front of the store. Caine led Finnley to the front doors—all glass.

He pulled her back and led her around to a small clothing section. "Put on this cap. Pull your hair up and stuff it inside. Shades and glasses. It's a simple disguise and might buy us some time."

They slipped out the front doors through the pharmacy employees and into the crowd. Caine suspected that the arsonists and shooters were now in the crowd watching, believing they were dead. Splitting up might add to their disguise, but he wouldn't risk leaving her alone. They held hands and hurried down the sidewalk as more people rushed toward the fire that was taking out downtown Emmons.

Once this was over and they were somewhere safe, he suspected she would feel the full impact of such a huge loss.

Caine continued to remain situationally aware, eyeing every shadow and every window. Up ahead was the Dodge Charger he'd parked a couple of blocks down. He regretted driving it today. It had drawn attention and even now, someone had stopped to peer inside.

Someone with bulky arms and the demeanor of a hired gunman.

Caine yanked Finnley back into the shadows of an alley, sensing danger was closing in like a tight net around them.

In the alley, Caine faced her, pressing her against the brick wall of the building. He leaned in close.

"They found my car," he whispered.

The way he said it… She could almost feel the enormous weight of guilt on him along with the fear. He was so close and smelled like a mixture of smoke and the masculine aftershave he wore. It made her head dizzy even in this potentially lethal situation. It didn't matter where she was or what she was doing, being close to Caine did strange things to her insides— even at the worst times. She couldn't shake the effect he had on her, nor did she want to. She couldn't free herself from the power he had over her.

She shook her head, cleared her mind and slipped away. Standing just a few inches away made a difference as she tried to comprehend his words.

"Wait… What are you saying?"

"My car. They're watching it. We can't take it, so we need to find another way out of here." He stepped close again but turned his back slightly to her, then tugged her along with him to look at the front and back alley, their only exits. "If we're caught in here, we can get trapped again. I'm calling Everly."

He leaned in so Finnley could hear the call too.

"I'm already on it," his sister replied. "I saw the local news and knew you were in trouble. I'm so grateful you're out of the building."

"Right. That's one obstacle of many. How do we get out of here? It feels like they're all over the place. Crawling around the town looking for us to make sure we didn't escape the fire."

"I can't get a vehicle in. The roads are blocked off to allow more firetrucks in. They're coming in from neighboring towns. The fire could take out an entire city block or more if not stopped."

Gracious. The entire city block. Finnley covered her mouth as tears flooded her eyes. Oh, no… Her town was being destroyed because of her. Because of her stubbornness. She hadn't wanted to run and hide. She'd wanted to stand strong in the face of danger and keep her father's legacy and his reputation going even in the face of his devastating secrets.

"What do you suggest?" Caine asked.

"I'm looking at images of the town right now. Can you hide somewhere? Hide for the next ten minutes and then get to that field at the end of town."

"That's all you've got?"

"I'm sorry, Caine. That's the fastest way out."

"It could be the most dangerous too."

"Our helicopter will fit in with the news choppers. Just blend in with the crowd and make your way to that end of town. We'll get you out of there."

He ended the call and glanced at the front alley again, looking perplexed instead of relieved.

"Why don't we go out the back? No one is back there except the firetrucks."

"Exactly. We'll stand out to anyone watching. Our only shot is to blend in with the crowd."

Tugging her hand, he led her to the corner and peered out and around. A group of people walked the sidewalk, rushing toward the taped-off area, and Caine pulled her with him into the group and picked up the pace to match their movements. They were all together. Wearing their caps and sunglasses, they merged into the next crowd the group approached.

Caine eased her along the sidewalk between people as they looked on in horror, cried and talked about the devastation. Finnley thought her heart would be crushed under the grief. She allowed a glance at the firemen spraying water on two buildings now.

Two. Buildings.

Mr. Patel's store would be destroyed too.

Her breath caught in her throat. Caine glanced back at her as if somehow sensing her grief. He said nothing, but she saw the compassion in his eyes and that he was also determined to get her to safety. He probably carried the burden of guilt for letting this happen when it was really her fault.

Then again, all the burden lay at the feet of these bad men, who'd come to destroy her life and take everything from her, including her father.

And maybe, yeah, maybe a lot of it rested at her father's feet. He'd already paid a high price. These thoughts swirled in her mind and took up too much space when she needed to focus on following Caine. He gripped her hand tightly, but then someone stepped in the way, and she had to tug free to keep from slamming into them. She hated the suffocating feeling of so many people surrounding her.

Caine caught up with her again.

They couldn't move too quickly. That would draw the wrong people's attention, and possibly even bring more harm to this crowd than half the city block burning.

Rebuild. You can rebuild.

But lives couldn't be replaced.

At the edge of the crowd on the opposite end of town, news crews had parked in a field and were headed this way. At least two helicopters had landed, but one took off again, and Caine stopped. She leaned closer and stood on her tiptoes to whisper in his ear. "What are we waiting on?"

"The moment when I should step out. Plus, Everly's helicopter needs to land first."

"How do you know which one it is."

"We share a lease with the town of West Ridge's PD for use. I've flown it. I'll recognize it." He squeezed her hand, reassuring her.

Like hers, his palm had become moist from too much heat and stress. She caught a glance of herself in the reflection of a vehicle's window. Could she look any worse? There were dark smudges all over her face, and her hair was falling out of the cap. If anyone after them saw her face, they would instantly know it was her. She and Caine were the only ones with smudges on their faces like they'd had to escape a fire. She subtly wiped at her face since everyone was focused on the firemen putting out the fire.

A shout rose from the crowd and many clapped and cheered.

Finnley tried to see past the big man in front and finally realized the fire had been doused, but not before both buildings had completely crumbled in on themselves, except for the brick portions, which were now blackened. She wanted to cheer too, but then again, if she had thought her life had been destroyed before, she'd been dead wrong.

She no longer had a home to return to. And no job, since her father's legacy had been destroyed.

She sagged under the weight of the pain and accidentally leaned against a man who had just stepped from the storefront behind them. When she glanced up at him, his eyes narrowed, and he slipped a gun out and into her side.

SIXTEEN

Caine sensed the atmosphere around them had shifted. The hairs on the back of his neck stood on end. Finnley gasped and stiffened. He palmed his gun. What was happening? Something was wrong.

I can't lose you.

I won't lose you.

Then he knew.

He didn't think.

He acted. Let his instincts kick in. He shoved the man's gun up and away from Finnley's side and slammed his hand into the man's trachea. The gun went off, shooting a hole in the wall, before clattering to the ground.

People screamed and scattered.

Not what Caine had wanted or expected. He grabbed the gun. No sense leaving it behind in case this guy was able to recover.

"Let's go!" He sprinted down the sidewalk.

If anyone was in place, watching and waiting to shoot, they were in trouble. But they were out of time. Pain shot up his leg, but adrenaline powered him through the agony. He ran, thinking to hold back so Finnley could keep up, but she suddenly sprinted forward and passed him, running faster than he could with the injured leg he'd earned from landing wrong on that jump from the building.

"Where are we going?" she shouted over her shoulder.

A helicopter was landing near the news chopper, but it suddenly shot up into the air and headed toward them, landing at the edge of the field near the town.

"That's Brett. Get in."

"I won't leave you behind."

"Get in, Finnley. I'll catch up."

He was slowing down significantly. His leg didn't hurt that badly. What was it? What was happening?

Caine suddenly sank to the ground. He couldn't make his body work. Nothing responded. Brett was at his side and shouldered him to his feet. Finnley was on the other side. They assisted him into the helicopter and strapped him in, and Brett took off. Finnley put on a headset and put one on Caine.

"Caine, what happened? What's wrong?"

He closed his eyes, feeling weaker by the second. He pressed his hand against his side where he suddenly felt pain, and when he lifted his fingers, they were covered in blood.

"Change of plans, Brett." He struggled to speak the rest. "I've...been...shot."

Finnley squeezed his hand. "This is all my fault, Caine. All my fault. I'm so sorry. I should have listened to you."

"Can you press your hand against his side?" Brett asked. "Against the gunshot wound. We have to stop the bleeding."

Caine should have thought of that. He should have thought to grab the gunshot wound powder from a medical supply pack somewhere in this helicopter.

Brett radioed ahead to the hospital, got permission to land and asked for emergency services to meet him.

Caine was barely aware they landed. The door swung open, and emergency personnel hefted him out of the helicopter and onto a gurney. Someone worked his side while an oxygen mask was placed over his face all while he was wheeled into the hospital.

How could he protect Finnley if he was down and out? *God, please keep her safe.*

Caine opened his eyes. Was he going to die? Why weren't they helping him? Why weren't they doing anything about the gunshot?

His sister appeared next to him. "Good. You're awake now. You went through surgery just fine. They've given us a few minutes with you in recovery."

"What? I… I had surgery?"

"Yes. They removed the bullet and patched you up. Luckily, no organs were hit."

He snagged Everly's hand, hating how weak his grip felt. "Keep Finnley safe."

"Don't worry, we've got this. You get better."

"I'll be back on the job soon."

"I know you want to be, but not until you're better."

A nurse came into the room, ushered the two women out and checked Caine's vitals.

Until this is over.

And when it was over, he didn't want her to leave. But today's gunshot incident was a perfect example of the life he lived and the danger. Finnley needed someone safer. Then again, Finnley was tied to a growing threat, just like Sophie had been.

"Can I get you anything?" the nurse asked.

"Yeah. You can get me out of here."

"I'm afraid that isn't happening anytime soon."

Soon was relative.

"I need to get out of here," he said. "Let me speak to the doctor."

At the Honor Protection Specialist headquarters, Finnley stared out the panoramic window at the view of Mount Rainier. She couldn't visit Caine just yet because she wasn't family. Each member of the Honor family had gone up to see him. Ayden planned to stay at the hospital until visiting hours were over.

Finnley felt numb all over.

Again.

She hadn't really recovered from her father's brutal murder, being pushed off a road and shot at multiple times, but now this... The shop and her home being torched while they were trapped inside... That was the proverbial icing on the cake. Icing was the completely wrong descriptor, but she wasn't in a place to waste time thinking of something better.

Finnley was sliding into a deep, dark hole, and if she finally slid all the way in, she wasn't entirely sure she could find her way out again. The fire chief had been in contact regarding the investigation, and she gave him all the details of what had happened.

Sheriff Henderson had come to the headquarters and taken her statement, and she guessed the woman had taken Caine's statement at the hospital.

"Now do you believe me?" Finnley had asked. "That my father was murdered?"

"Finnley, I'm sorry that I discounted your thoughts at first, but I long ago decided that your father's death is suspicious. An FBI agent has been assigned to look into his death, and we're cooperating with that agency as well as the ATF regarding his...um...storage unit." Sheriff Henderson slightly shook her head, revealing her absolute surprise at this turn of events that could implicate her father, a man no one suspected of being anything but kind and generous.

"Funny. Nobody has talked to me about it yet."

"I'm sure they will. But you've been through quite a shock today. I advise you to rest while you can. You're in good hands with this protection agency, so please stay with them until we capture the people behind this."

Finnley was glad when Sheriff Henderson left. Everly peeked from the door across the large open space. "Can I come in?"

"Of course. This is your place, not mine."

Finnley didn't look at her. She just stared at the mountain, watching the clouds and haze move in to obscure the view. She suspected that most of the haze was due to the smoke from the Emmons downtown fire, as it was being called via broadcast news stations.

Everly sat in the plush seat catty-corner from Finnley on the sofa, and she stared out the window as well. She said nothing. Maybe she was simply waiting for Finnley to talk. Finnley didn't want to talk.

Or…maybe she did. Yeah, she did. "Everything is destroyed."

"I'm so sorry," Everly said.

Finnley could hear the sincerity in her voice.

"I mean any remaining evidence," Finnley said. "I think that's why they did it, don't you?"

"I can't be sure, but that could be one reason."

"I don't know who Frank Wilbanks was. That's all I want right now. I want to know who my father really was, his true identity, and I want to know who *I* am."

"I'm sure your father—no matter his past—was only trying to protect you. Whatever he was hiding, it was for you, and the man he presented to you, is the man he was. Our jobs that we do are not who we are."

Caine had said something similar about her father. "Then what defines who we are?"

Everly seemed to think about her answer and then finally said, "The people we love. The actions we take to love them. You know that about your father. That… That's who he was, Finnley. You need to trust that. There is the old saying that actions speak louder than words. But even then, if they aren't done in love, they mean nothing in the end. It's just a lot of noise."

"You're talking about the Bible. The scripture in Corinthians, aren't you?"

"Yes. If I *'have not charity, I am become as sounding brass, or a tinkling cymbal.'*"

"I think Dad definitely had love. I have no doubt about that. That's why none of this makes any sense."

Everly nodded. "Caine told me about the people at the funeral. They all loved your father, so I know he did good deeds sincerely and with love."

Finnley soaked in the words and tried to take them to heart. She'd known that before, but somehow, as they had slowly uncovered more mysteries behind her father's identities, she'd lost sight of it.

"But do you believe he might have been involved in something illicit? What about that? Doesn't that erase everything else?" Finnley asked.

"Let's not jump to conclusions. Instead, let's wait to learn the truth. Even if we don't like what we find, I believe the man you knew was true and good and perhaps trying to right the past wrongs. He could have been working for good all along, and that's what I believe. You should choose to believe it too."

"What does Caine think? I know he talks to you. Tells you things he doesn't tell me."

"Caine believes your father worked for a government agency—that's my belief too—and that his identity needs to remain secret. For your safety, of course, but also for the safety and security of others."

"Then why does someone want to kill me?"

"Obviously, someone knows who your father was."

"And they want to silence me too," Finnley said. "They think I know something."

Everly moved to sit close to her and took her hand. "I know

it's a lot to take in, but you need to give your heart and mind a rest. The authorities are looking into this, and because you hired us, we're looking into it too. I promise we'll find the truth. We'll learn who he was, and we'll stop the men after you. You have to trust the process and be patient. Finnley, look at me."

Finnley shifted her gaze from Mount Rainier but said nothing.

"Promise me you'll get some rest. We have the theater, remember? You watched a movie the other night. You could watch old movies. I'll watch with you. Eat popcorn and relax."

"While Caine is in the hospital?"

"You aren't helping Caine sitting here and going to this dark place. He wouldn't want to see you like this. I'm asking you to do this for you as much as for Caine. When we see him again, I want you to be healthy, and for him to know that we took good care of you. Can you do this for Caine?"

For Caine.

Later that evening, after she and Everly had watched an old Charlton Heston movie, Finnley yawned and headed for her room. She grabbed the clothes she'd shed after the fire to put in the hamper. She'd ask about where to do the laundry tomorrow. By force of habit, she emptied all the pockets. One time, she'd inadvertently washed her cell phone, and it had been useless after that.

In her jacket pocket, she found the slip of paper that Mrs. Tomlinson had given her.

SEVENTEEN

Two days later, Caine was relieved to be back at headquarters.

"You need to go home and rest. I'm your boss, and that's what I'm telling you to do." Ayden stood at the main entrance where they received clients.

Brett had brought Caine from the hospital to headquarters as soon as Caine had been able to pressure the doctor enough to release him. He'd explained he could get more rest at home, that he was on the mend, so why keep him in the hospital? He had a feeling that Dr. Sax was only letting him think he'd made a difference with his nagging. He probably would have gone home today anyway.

Still, he had to keep an eye on the wound to make sure it was healing correctly. No big deal. Not like he hadn't been through this before.

"We're all partners in this business, bro," Caine said to Ayden. "I'm back to work on light duty. I need to see Finnley."

"She's in good hands." Ayden crossed his arms.

Caine pushed past his brother.

"What?" Ayden asked. "You don't trust us to take care of a client? Or is there something more going on between you two?" Ayden sent him the squiggly eye, and Caine wasn't sure if he was kidding or serious.

"You might want to get that checked." Caine gestured at Ayden's strange eyebrow movements.

Ayden followed Caine down the hall. "Caine, listen." His brother's kidding tone had disappeared. "She's a client. You know the rules."

Caine had had enough. He turned on his brother to stand his ground. "Seriously? You mean the same rules you followed with your old flame Hannah? The same rules Everly followed with Sawyer? And Brett with Kinsley?"

Ayden averted his gaze and scratched his forehead. "Right. Rules are meant to be broken." He stared at Caine, reading him. "Is she important to you?"

Caine hung his head. "Yes. She's important." Then he lifted his face to make sure Ayden could read the sincerity in his eyes. The seriousness of this. "But nothing can happen between us. Don't make it a thing. Am I clear?"

"Crystal," Ayden said.

Caine turned and pressed forward, trying to hide his grunts of pain. He hadn't taken the pain medication because he needed to be completely alert. It wasn't that long ago that Finnley had taken some pain meds because of the graze on her arm, and she had been kind of loopy. And cute. But Caine didn't want to be either. He found Finnley in Everly's office looking at the large span of monitors.

Finnley slowly lifted her gaze to his, and her eyes widened with her gasp. "Caine!"

She jumped from the chair and raced over to him but pulled back at the last moment. "I don't want to hurt you."

He grinned, feeling the rush of emotion and care he had for this woman. This tender woman who had gotten under his skin and into his heart. He reached for her and gently pulled her against him. Kissed the top of her head and breathed in the scent of her. It would break his heart once he had to let her go.

But he would.

He would let her go.

Even if he let himself fall for her after his resolve never

to love again after Sophie, Finnley deserved a world without danger. A life without danger. Caine couldn't give her that, and this situation with her had only proved it, confirmed to him that Finnley deserved someone…safer.

Throats cleared, and Finnley stepped back, her face a pretty shade of pink. Ayden, Brett and Everly stood watching.

"I'm so glad you're back," Finnley said. "But how did they let you out so soon?"

"The gunshot just nicked a muscle. No organs. I'm healing fast and fine. I've been through much worse. Nothing for me to do at the hospital I can't do at home."

"But you're not *home*." Of course, Ayden would have to point that out.

Fine. Caine wasn't backing down. "This is home for now."

Caine shot him a glare. *Shut up. Not in front of Finnley.*

He tried to move smoothly and appear like he wasn't in pain as he made his way around to sit next to Everly, who'd returned to her computer monitors. She'd been watching Caine and Finnley with those eagle eyes of hers. He expected to get a lecture at some point.

"What have we learned?" he asked.

She shared a look with Ayden as if getting his go-ahead, which angered Caine. He didn't need Ayden's permission. As for Everly, he understood her perspective.

Let's keep Ayden happy so we can all get along.

"A couple of things, actually." She typed on her keyboard to bring up video from the Emmons Budget Storage incident.

"Which are?"

"Okay. The secret office and the storage with guns and other electronics made us suspect that he's a field operative."

"English please," Finnley said.

"In the movies, CIA operatives are often called agents. Any agent from any agency can be called that, but they go by other names. A CIA employee is called an officer, and anyone they handle is called an operative."

"Wait, are you saying my father was CIA?"

"I'm not saying anything. Just using that as an example. I believe he was an intelligence officer—either an analyst or an operative—for a government agency."

"What is the difference, and why do you think this?"

Ayden crossed his arms. "Why analyst, Everly? With everything we've seen, it seems more like he was someone deeply planted for fieldwork."

"Okay, just stop." Caine didn't want to tell them they were making his head spin. "All of this is conjecture. What exactly do you *know*?" There. Cut to the chase.

"Nothing. I keep running into brick walls. And that in itself is a red flag. If I can't dig deeper than the obvious, his true identity is hidden and requires security clearance." Everly looked at Ayden. "Do you still have connections? Ayden used to have security clearance as a diplomatic security agent because he worked to protect high-value targets," Everly explained.

"Excuse me," Finnley said. "What is a high-value target?"

"I need to give you some thriller novels to read, Finnley," his sister teased, then her mouth dropped. "Maybe this isn't the best time to joke around. My apologies for being insensitive."

"It's fine. I'm up for a thriller novel if that will help me understand my father's world better. I think I get why he pushed me more toward the classics and literature and academics. The past. He didn't want me to read about the spy world and get any ideas."

Caine nodded. "That's a thought."

"I can contact my connections and see what I can come up with," Ayden said.

"Thanks." Everly turned to her computer monitor. "In the meantime, it would seem that he learned something that put him in danger. Maybe he was stocking up, securing the necessary firearms. I don't know. But I see him as an analyst. This reminds me of that old Robert Redford movie." She looked at each one of them.

"Oh." Brett snapped his fingers repeatedly. "I know the one."

"*Three Days of the Condor*," Everly said.

Finnley leaned forward. "What's it about?"

Caine didn't like that Everly had brought that up. It didn't exactly end well for anyone near the main character. "Let me." He stared at Everly, hoping she understood that he wanted to leave out the graphic details. Her expression softened, and she nodded.

"I think it reminds Everly of this situation because the main character was a quiet, bookish guy," Caine said. "He read books all day at work. That's the main connection, right, Everly?" He again shared a look with her, sending her a message. This was far too much information for Finnley, and again, it was all conjecture. But often investigators worked with a theory. Everly was simply sharing her own, and Ayden had asked for it. Caine had asked for it.

"But there's more?" Finnley held his gaze as if challenging him to tell her everything.

"Unfortunately, yes. He read books for the CIA, searching for hidden messages." He leaned back and looked at his sister. "You said that you had a couple of new things. What's the other thing?"

He did not want to continue and tell her that when the main character got home from lunch one day, everyone in the office had been killed because he had stumbled upon a scenario that his own agency, the CIA, didn't want anyone to know about.

"So they killed them all?" Finnley asked.

See? This was a bad idea. He nodded.

He hoped and prayed that this wasn't a similar scenario, and that Frank's agency wasn't trying to silence not only him but everyone around him. Maybe Frank had found a way to hide and keep his head down in Emmons. Until they knew more, Finnley would be looking over her shoulder. After he heard from Everly, he would bring up Mrs. Tomlinson. With everything that had happened, he had forgotten about her. No one had mentioned that anyone had died in the incident. So she must have survived, which meant she likely had some skills. Just more confirmation that they needed to look closely at her.

"I'm waiting, Everly. What else have you got? And I hope it's more than a theory."

"Finnley can share the rest," Everly said. "Go ahead. Tell him, Finnley."

Finnley had been thinking about this ever since she found the slip of paper in her pocket. And she'd made a decision she didn't think anyone in this room would like. Still, she'd hired them, and she could fire them. But really, she didn't want to do that. She wanted them to work with her.

Finnley moved to sit in the chair next to Caine. "That day that Mrs. Tomlinson came back. Do you remember?"

"Yes." It was just two days ago, in fact, but he would keep that to himself.

"She knocked on the door and insisted that we let her in. I opened the door and she—"

Now. He remembered more. "Stuck something in your hand. Whispered something to you," Caine said. "I remember."

Finnley nodded. "But with everything happening so fast, I never got to tell you. I didn't even remember until I was cleaning out the pockets of my clothes. I found the slip of paper she handed me. I'm so glad I stuck it in my pocket, or I know I would have lost it in our great escape."

"What did it say?"

"Three simple words." She hesitated.

"Here." Everly showed him the paper that she'd secured in a clear evidence baggie.

"'Take the cruise,'" he read out loud. He looked up at his siblings and then at Finnley. "Take the cruise?"

Everly nodded. "What do you make of that, Finnley?"

"I can tell you what I make of it. She knows something." Caine scraped a hand through his hair. "The woman caught my attention the first time she came into the store. Her complete shock at hearing about Frank's death and her reaction wasn't out of the ordinary, but I don't know… There was just something about the way she spoke to Finnley, and then of course, the shooting right after. I say it's time to get busy. This is a lead. Let's follow it." He directed his next words to Finnley. "You said that your father had planned for you guys to head to Seattle several days early, before the cruise. When were you supposed to leave?"

"It's two days from now. It's a cruise through the Inside Passage."

"And this Mrs. Tomlinson knew about the cruise. Do you know anything about her, like her first name or what kind of vehicle she drives? Where she lives?" Everly asked Finnley. She appeared to be searching the name Tomlinson in the area, coming up with hundreds of hits.

Finnley hated the fact that she knew so little. "No, I'm sorry," she said. "She was just a customer. She doesn't live in town. I knew that much. She'd come in every couple of months."

"What did she buy?" Caine asked. "Maybe that will tell us something."

"I didn't pay too much attention. By all appearances, she was just a friend, a well-dressed woman who visited the shop occasionally. Dad always perked up with he saw her, but he was like that with a lot of people." She should have paid more attention. Asked more questions.

"Humor me, please," he said. "Do you remember what she bought?"

"Oh, right. Stationery. Something different every time. But it seemed she always wanted to chat with Dad. Now that I think about it, I could easily see that was her main purpose in coming. She wasn't there for the stationery." Finnley should have known. She should have seen it when it mattered.

"She knew him," Caine said. "I'm betting she knows what's going on."

Finnley stood. She had to do this. "I agree. That's why I'm going on that cruise."

"What?" Caine stood too. "No, you can't. Finnley, let us handle this. You were almost killed. Multiple attempts to either take you, harm you or kill you have been made. I won't allow it."

"You won't allow it? How about I get to make the decisions about what I'm doing."

"You hired me. You hired *us* to protect you. Let us do it. We can learn what's going on without you having to leave the security of our headquarters."

"He's right," Ayden said. "You need to remain in a safe location."

She looked from Ayden to Brett to Everly and then back to Caine. They were all ganging up on her. "I understand your concern. I do. But Mrs. Tomlinson, or whoever she is, is not going to talk to any of you. She told me to take the cruise. Maybe she wants to keep me safe, or maybe she wants to tell me who my father really was. She knows what's going on. Maybe it's everything."

"Maybe it's none of that." Brett lifted a shoulder.

Wrong answer. "I'm hungry, and I'm going to raid your kitchen pantry. Why don't you guys have a family confab without me. I know you want to talk about it out of my earshot. Nothing is going to change my mind. I need to get packed and ready for a cruise, though, and so I hope you're going to help me with that. I appreciate you letting me stay here, because right now I have nowhere else to go. So that's kind of why I don't want to fire you." She hung her head and then lifted it to Caine. "You've protected me so far, kept me alive, and you're all working hard on getting answers. I trust you to keep doing this, but you need to let me have a say. After all, isn't the customer always right?"

She sighed heavily. "The thing is…learning who my father really was is everything to me. Nothing else matters. I can't move on until I have the answer. If I find out who he was, really, then I can know who I am. Don't you get that?" She shrugged. "I'm doing this with or without your help. But I'd prefer if you're in it with me."

She turned and left them with that. At the kitchen table, she ended up drinking a plain glass of water. Her outburst had deflated her, but at least she'd put her foot down and let them know her decision. She hadn't wanted them to see how very afraid she was.

Slumped at the kitchen table, the wall at the back was in full view. She read the scripture written in huge scripted letters that took up half the wall. She hadn't come all the way into the kitchen since she'd been here, so she hadn't had an occasion to see it.

"Be not afraid; only believe." Mark 5:36.

Yes. That was exactly what she needed.

EIGHTEEN

Caine squeezed his eyes shut.

What just happened?

"Why didn't you tell me?" He opened his eyes and glared at Everly. "You should have told me. She has had this time to make the decision to go on that cruise. If you had told me, I could have talked her through it the moment she found that piece of paper in her pocket."

"Caine, just settle down. You were in the hospital recovering. As far as I'm concerned, you shouldn't even be here. You need to trust us with this. You need to rest."

"She's right, Caine." Ayden stepped forward. "I can see the pain in your face. You can't fool me."

"The pain in my face is because I'm afraid for Finnley. We cannot let her go on that cruise. This is ridiculous."

He got up and lumbered down the hall, passed Finnley in the kitchen and then found the room he usually took when staying at headquarters. They each had their own homes, but they also had space here. This big warehouse had been renovated to include everything they needed, including accommodations when protecting clients. They also had everything that maybe they didn't need but wanted—like a basketball court, full workout facility, theater and library.

Caine crashed on the bed. Maybe he should take some pain meds, after all.

God, help me. I can't do this without You. I need to finish this. All I can think about is how I failed Sophie. I saw that car racing toward her. I should have gotten to her sooner. Shoved her out of the way in time to save her. But I didn't. And she died. I've learned to let that go and not blame myself, but if something happens to Finnley... How could I live with myself?

God, I need You. I need You so much. I need You above all else.

Peace finally settled on him. He hadn't felt it so strong in so very long, but he embraced it and let himself rest.

Sleep.

A gentle knock came at the door, and Caine stirred awake. Wow. He hadn't meant to sleep for two whole hours. He sat up on the bed and tried to compose himself, shoving past the dizziness. He was okay. He would be fine. He was healing. He just had to watch out for infection. He was on antibiotics. Maybe he should change his dressing now.

The knock came again. "Caine, it's me."

Finnley.

He stood and opened the door.

She glanced up at his hair and then down his body. "Oh, I woke you. I'm sorry." She turned to walk away.

He snagged her wrist and dragged her inside. She smiled. He loved that smile.

He sat back on the bed. "Have a seat."

She took the lone chair, and her eyes snagged on his hair again.

"I have bed head, huh?"

"Yeah. How are you feeling?"

"Good."

"You're lying."

"It'll take time. But I'm a soldier, and I can soldier through."

"No one is asking you to."

He stared at her. "Ouch. That hurt." Maybe he shouldn't have said that out loud.

"I don't mean it like that. I don't mean it like I don't want you to soldier through or be part of my protection detail. I want you, Caine, but I want you to be okay. To be healthy and safe. You risked your life for me. I'll forever be grateful."

He got a sinking feeling. "Is that it then? Is that what you came in to tell me? You're saying goodbye? Firing me?"

"What? No." Flustered, she stood. "I'm terrible at communicating. Caine, listen to me. I have an idea. I wanted you to hear it first."

Okay. Well, that sounded much better. His heart rate slowed a little. He really shouldn't let this woman get so close to him that if she dumped his protection, he would get this upset. But it was already too late.

"Well, have a seat again. Relax. I'm listening."

"I know you all must think I'm like a really stupid heroine in a dumb movie that goes into the dark basement alone. You know—too stupid to live so she deserves to die."

"What? Of course, we don't think that. No, that's not it at all."

"Well, I've given you reason to look at me like that by telling you I'm going on that cruise. But you have to admit that I need to be there. Mrs. Tomlinson, or anyone else who is there, is only going to talk to *me*. Not you. Me. Because this is about *my* father. She doesn't know you. So I have a plan. Why don't all of you come with me on the cruise, and you can work undercover and protect me that way."

Huh. He closed his eyes. *That's a good plan.* Honestly, he couldn't believe he hadn't thought of it, then again, he was recovering from a gunshot wound. He'd bet that Everly had already thought of it.

"Did you… Have you already talked to Everly about this?"

"What? No. She's out shopping for me right now."

Fury surged in his gut that Everly would already be assisting Finnley in this crazy idea. Still, Everly was probably working to keep Finnley close while she formulated a plan.

"That's a good idea. And since you've already made up your mind to go, we're going with you. My guess is that we'll have to clear our schedules if other clients are waiting."

"Oh. I hadn't thought of that. Well, this should take, what, a day? I mean, once I'm there, the answer should come quickly."

"If there are answers. If this plays out like we hope. But, Finnley, after everything we've been through, all our careful plans that have gone wrong, you have to know that this will be dangerous."

"Look, I feel like Mrs. Tomlinson wouldn't have risked her life—because she really did—if this wasn't important. Those bullets were flying quickly there. She was desperate to tell me to go on the cruise. She knows something. She's going to be there."

"We have a lot to work through. A lot to figure out. Let me clean up and get everyone together so we can figure out our undercover protection detail."

Finnley stood, her eyes glistening with gratitude, and, man, he wanted to hold her. To kiss her. He wished they were somewhere else, and that danger wasn't chasing them. He wished he could be free to love her.

In Finnley's new but temporary room at HPS headquarters, she went through the sacks of clothes that Everly had bought, folded and stuck in her new luggage. No time for washing before wearing. Really, she didn't have the energy or care enough to wash them first.

This was really happening.

"You really went overboard, Everly. I promise I'll pay you back." Once she figured out the insurance on the burned-up store. She hadn't had time to even think about her finances or her future.

Everly smiled. "You're going on a cruise, and you need to look like you mean it. Like this is real."

"Except everyone who knows about it knows it isn't for real. My father—"

"Bought you the tickets. You're taking this cruise as a tribute to him, in memory of him and the time you should have spent together. You need this cruise to get away."

"Okay, but the truth is, this isn't going to feel remotely like a getaway for me." She dropped another cute but warm outfit—this wasn't a Caribbean cruise—into the luggage and faced Everly. "I'm doing this. I have to. But I don't mind being honest with you." She held Everly's gaze.

"You're scared."

"Yes."

"I would think something was wrong with you if you weren't," Everly said. "I'll be honest with you too. This isn't how we like to run operations. Putting a client in the center of danger... You should know that I was able to get access to the manifest, and Mrs. Tomlinson isn't registered as a passenger, at least, not under that name, if she is going to be there at all."

"I'm in the center of danger regardless. You didn't put me there. And I believe that Mrs. Tomlinson is trying to help me."

A knock came at the door. "It's Caine."

"Come in," both Everly and Finnley called.

He opened the door, his eyes flashing at his sister. What was up with that? He seemed irritated with her.

"You all packed, Everly?" Caine asked.

Finnley got the distinct impression he wanted to talk to her alone.

"Yes," Everly said. "As are Brett and Ayden. We have a plan in place. Secured the tickets. Hannah will stay here to run things and take care of you, Caine."

"I secured a ticket too." Caine struggled to keep a smirk from his lips. "And I'm packed too."

Everly fisted her hands on her hips. "I thought we agreed that you aren't in any condition to go. You need to stay home and recover."

"No. We didn't agree. Finnley needs someone right by her side. Mrs. Tomlinson has seen me, so she knows I'm with Finnley. I'm going."

Finnley rushed to his side and grabbed his hand. Warmth surged through her, but concern filled her heart. "Are you sure?" The question was almost a whisper. "I couldn't bear it if something…"

He held her gaze, and she could have stood there forever and stared in his eyes. They had such a strong connection, and she didn't want to let go of his hand. She wished they were going on a cruise together for far different reasons.

"Yes. I'm sure. I'm going to be there for you until the end, Finnley."

Until the end.

She'd heard those words before, and the reminder sent a rush of fear through her. A good reminder that every man she'd trusted, every man she'd loved, had hurt her. Even…even her father. She stepped back. He hadn't meant it as in forever. More like until this investigation was over.

Moving back to the luggage, she focused on packing.

"Since Finnley and I are sharing a room, we'll be friends on the cruise, Caine," Everly said. "You really didn't need to do this. But I understand it's hard to think clearly with your emotions all caught up in your client." Everly stomped out of the room.

Wow. Everly was really upset that Caine had decided to go, but there was more to it. She'd mentioned that Caine's emotions were caught up with her, the same as she was caught up in him emotionally. Romantically. Despite their previous discussion. Regardless of the fact that they were both emotionally damaged. Everly saw it, which meant that Finnley and

Caine were not doing a very good job resisting whatever was between them.

A pang ricocheted through her heart, and she looked at Caine. "I didn't mean to cause problems between you and your siblings."

"You didn't. We're family. Stuff happens, and we get over it." He eased into the chair. "So you understand the plan, right? You just act normal—"

"That's just it. What is normal? My father was just murdered. My shop just burned down." She fought the tears. *Do not cry.* "See what I'm saying? What is normal?"

He blew out a breath and then slowly approached her.

She held her breath. When he got near like this, she couldn't breathe.

"That's a good question. Just be true to yourself, Finnley. You've been through a lot. Whatever you're feeling while on the cruise, just be you."

She dipped her head. Whatever she was feeling? Right now, she wanted to be in his arms. She swallowed. Her whole body trembled. Did he know? Did he see what he did to her? How was she going to go on this cruise with Caine? Her body had a mind of its own, and she leaned a little forward, and he was there with his arms around her. She nestled into his chest.

"Ah, careful." He shifted slightly.

"Oh, I didn't mean to hurt you."

"It's okay." He snuggled her against his chest. "I'll protect you with my life, Finnley."

"I don't want you to do that," she said. "I want us to both come out of this alive."

The timbre of his chuckle sounded in his chest. "That's the plan. I'm only saying you can trust me completely."

He stepped back and lifted her chin, forcing her to look into his hazel eyes. "You can trust me…with everything."

Oh…

NINETEEN

You can trust me with everything? What in the world had he been thinking telling her that. Really, he only meant to reassure her about the cruise. He knew she was scared. He'd felt her trembling in his arms.

Or did her reaction have to do with something else?

Thoughts of her, memories of that moment, needed to take a back seat so he could focus on the plan they'd made. Everly drove Caine and Finnley to the dock where they would get on the cruise ship.

Brett and Ayden took their own rides, so they would appear as separate parties. Finnley and Everly were rooming together for Finnley's protection, and it was decided that Caine would go as her boyfriend.

Not her protector.

But come on, any boyfriend worth his mettle was a protector. The thing was, he kind of felt like he didn't have to pretend in that role. He knew Everly was onto him. She kept giving him that disapproving look.

Whatever.

They boarded the cruise ship to Alaska, which was just a big hotel on the water. Caine had never actually been on a cruise, though Ayden had. That was where he'd proposed to Hannah. Everyone had someone to love. Everyone but Caine.

The big floating hotel slowly pulled away from port, and

Caine went to the upper deck. Sports deck, maybe? He was wrong. This was much bigger and more complex than a hotel. They were going to have to work hard to keep up with Finnley.

He'd spotted Brett and Ayden checking out all the various ways that this could go wrong. They hadn't had as much time as they wanted to prepare for this operation, and Ayden wasn't happy with it, but sometimes you just had to work with what you had.

Finnley and Everly were supposed to meet Caine up on the deck.

Well, I'm here? Where are you?

He could ask them using the same earpieces that the U.S. Secret Service used. They were all wearing them covered with hats or scarves.

He turned when someone approached. Wearing a gimme cap and a plain rain jacket, Ayden leaned over the rail to look out over Puget Sound and watch the cityscape go by.

"You can trust me with everything? Really, Caine?"

How had Ayden known? Someone had been listening in to his conversation with Finnley, and he would bet that someone was Everly.

"I'm sorry, do I know you?" Caine asked. "I'm waiting on my girlfriend."

Ayden chuckled and strolled away. If Caine was here, then Brett was covering Finnley and Everly from a distance. He turned his back to the water and scenery so he could watch the people and yet look relaxed and like he was excited to be here.

Finally, Finnley and Everly appeared on the deck. They smiled and laughed, and Finnley couldn't look more beautiful in a pink jacket and white beanie that emphasized her big brown eyes.

Images of Sophie dressed for an evening out in Italy rushed through his mind, and weirdly, for the first time, the familiar pain at those memories didn't crush him. The memory faded on its own without bringing more grief, and Finnley's smile filled his mind.

No. No, no. He could not let her replace Sophie. He'd held on to Sophie's memory for so long. But…maybe it was time to let go of her completely. As Finnley's brilliant smile took his breath away, he had a feeling he didn't have a choice.

"There you are," Finnley said.

Finnley rushed forward, and like a skilled undercover worker, she slipped her arm around him, avoiding his injury. Then she tipped her head up and kissed him gently on the lips.

Everly cleared her throat. "Careful now. No need to enjoy this cruise too much."

She had tried to warn him away, and maybe she'd been right.

"We're working. This isn't fun at all." He smiled down at Finnley and winked.

She sent him a knowing look. They were on the same page, which he never really doubted, because they had shared moments. Connections. He was going to break both their hearts when this was over.

Pain—the heartfelt kind—surged inside, and he looked away. Instead of eagle or hawk or raven for a code name, they decided to simply call Tomlinson Mrs. T. Good enough.

"Any sight of Mrs. T?"

"Nope." Ayden.

"Negative." Brett. "But I saw a couple of guys that remind me of feds."

Interesting. "Everly? Any sight of Mrs. T?"

"I haven't received any information or intel about suspicious passengers—good guys or bad guys."

Great. Caine held his elbow out, and Finnley put her hand in. "Let's go for a cruise around this ship."

"Don't forget I'm here," his sister said. "I'm right behind you. Watching every move."

"Like a chaperone."

"Guys, can you dial it down," Finnley said. "This isn't help-ing anyone. Caine and I are playing a role. Nothing is real here."

Right. Could have fooled him. Her words hurt. She seemed so genuine. But really, he should tell himself this was all pre-tend. That was for the best. When they made it through this—whatever happened after this cruise—Caine needed to have a heart-to-heart with her. Be honest with himself and with her. He cared about her deeply.

I might even love her.

Just thinking it sent crazy surges of electricity all over him and made his heart tumble around inside. He stopped to take in the view. "Oh, look at that. It's Mount Baker."

"The San Juan Islands are on the other side."

"Listen, Everly. Move over there. I need to talk to Finnley." This cruise was putting pressure on them. Pushing them close and into a position for the lines of reality and pretend to blur. Finnley had said it was all pretend, but he wasn't sure that was true for either of them. He should have this talk with her be-fore it was too late and both of them ended up hurt.

"Really, Caine? Is now the time?" Everly asked. His sister was super protective of them all, and he wouldn't fault her for it, but sometimes she could be a pain.

"Yes. Really." He removed his earpiece so he wouldn't acci-dentally share his words with everyone. Finnley did the same.

"Caine, what is it?" Finnley's eyes shimmered. She shiv-ered in a sudden gust of wind. "I might have preferred a tropi-cal cruise to this."

Cute. She was trying to change the subject.

"Look at me. Please, look at me."

She shook her head and tears surged in her eyes. Oh. He didn't want to hurt her.

"Finnley, you drew a line in the sand before. You told me this can't happen. Do you remember saying that?"

A look of regret and deep sadness filled her eyes as she slowly nodded.

"I'm going to honor that. I'm *trying* to honor that."

Her lips flattened, and then she said, "But what if I've changed my mind?"

He hadn't expected that. Maybe it was already too late, and they were both much too vulnerable to think clearly. "*Did* you change your mind?"

"I don't know. I just know that I've been through a couple of breakups." She swiped at her eyes. "The last time, I was so stupid. I didn't see the signs. I didn't let myself believe that anyone could use me like that. Date me. Kiss me. Lead me on, and then do the same with three other women behind my back. I realize I'm not anything special. Not beautiful. Not really. Because of all that, I told myself I wouldn't fall for you. I couldn't let myself fall. I don't want to get hurt again. Are you going to hurt me, Caine?"

Oh. Man. She was so wrong. She was the most beautiful woman he'd ever seen—on the inside and outside—and she'd healed him of his past pain and loss. He'd already hurt her. Hurt them both. Even as he decided he could finally let himself love, he couldn't overcome the fact that she didn't deserve the kind of life he led. The danger factor.

She'd been through enough already. Caine cared enough about her that he wouldn't put her through more. And he would make it clear. Pain lanced through him as he pressed on, "You told me that there couldn't be anything between us. *You* made that choice. The truth is you don't want me. I'm not good for you. You've had a front-row seat, and you see what my job is like, don't you? See how dangerous it is?"

"What's happening now is because of my life, not yours."

"But as protection detail, this is what I do. I spend an inordinate amount of time with individuals to protect them. If not you, then someone else." And oh, man, it felt so wrong to say that. He hadn't meant to say it in such a way that she would think—

"Are you saying that you…you're like this…close like this, so connected…with everyone you protect?"

No. Oh, no. Never.

But she didn't wait for an answer and rushed away from him.

Finnley rushed through to the other side of the massive deck as fast as she could to get away from Caine. She needed a moment to herself without him trying to explain away what he'd just said to her. She didn't care if anyone paid attention to her. Most people were captivated by the beauty of the landscape and the amazing cruise ship anyway.

Her reaction to his little speech was so stupid. Not part of the plan at all. She was not supposed to be alone. But right now, she couldn't be with Caine.

"Finnley," he called after her.

Oh, man. He was coming after her. She glanced around the sea of people. Where could she go to get some space. She entered a big corridor, weaving through those who were trying to get on the deck with a view.

Of course, Caine's sister, looking none too happy, walked straight toward her from the opposite direction. Wow. She was like a spy on steroids. She must have memorized the floor plan on the ship's multiple decks. Or at least she had predicted Finnley would take this path, and she'd been waiting for her here.

The woman was strategic and was now heading Finnley off. Fine. She'd get lost on her own anyway. This place was a maze. Everly stood in her path, blocking her.

Heart pounding, Finnley tried to push past her as she asked, "What are you doing? Did you tag me or something?"

Everly smiled and pointed at Finnley's bag hanging over her shoulder. "Your purse has a tracker on it. I thought you knew."

Grabbing Finnley's arm, Everly turned her around to walk back out into the open and up on the sports deck with the other passengers. "Good show, putting on a fight," Everly said. "You guys should be apart for a while."

"You're enjoying this, aren't you? You want us to be apart." Finnley was such a fool, letting Caine get to her like that. Her heart was going to break at the absolute worst time. She couldn't breathe and gasped for breath.

Everly gently ushered her forward at a natural pace and squeezed her arm a little hard, as if trying to snap some sense into her. "Now, you listen to me. This is as dangerous as it gets. You insisted we do this, and now you need to stick to the plan or you're going to get yourself or Caine or one of us killed. Do you hear me?"

Finnley said nothing and worked hard to compose herself as she walked next to the woman. Everly had every reason to speak to her in that tone. She was absolutely right. Finnley had acted the fool over and over again. She wasn't sure if she could salvage the mess she'd made, though Everly could probably do it for her.

But that wasn't right.

They exited the hallway into a fine art gallery, and Everly strolled with her. Just two friends admiring the paintings.

"I made a mistake." She spoke so only Everly could hear. "I can't do this." She stopped walking and dragged in a deep breath. "I want to leave now."

But getting off a cruise ship in the middle of the journey wouldn't be so easy.

Everly gently pulled her into a hug and whispered, "I think Mrs. Tomlinson is here. Let's finish this, and then you never have to see Caine again."

Those words startled her. All of them. She wiped her eyes and stepped back. "What? Where?"

"Shh. Act natural. You're upset, and you don't have to hide

that. Let's go reel her in." Finnley walked with Caine's sister, a woman she was starting to consider a friend. But how well could she trust any of them? They were all just working. She was their client.

But she knew clients and customers could become friends. Just like Dad and Mrs. Tomlinson.

"Let's go above deck and play a game. That can give her the opportunity to engage." Everly was sharp.

Back on the sports deck, Everly leaned in and smiled. "Laugh at my joke. Don't look, she's watching you. I want you to head over to the shuffleboard game and act like you need a partner. I'm going to the restroom. See if she approaches. I'll stay close. Know that everyone is protecting you."

Finnley laughed like she was told. "I'll see you later, then," Finnley said in a normal voice, hoping Mrs. T heard.

Everly walked away, and Finnley strolled through the games, trying to decide which one to try. Though she struggled to play her part, she just settled into the fact that she didn't have to pretend. She was sad. Upset. Angry. Dad had died. And this thing with Caine was tying her in knots. She'd told herself repeatedly that they would go their separate ways. She'd lied to herself so she wouldn't get hurt and caused the very thing she'd tried to avoid.

She picked up a Ping-Pong paddle and considered it. She glanced around.

A woman grabbed the paddle on the opposite side.

Finnley was about to tell her no, that she was waiting for someone, when she looked up and gasped.

The woman laughed. "Come on. Let's play."

Mrs. T? Her breaths quickened. The woman had transformed her appearance, and Finnley hadn't recognized her. Wow. How had she changed her look so much? How had Everly spotted her so quickly?

"I'm glad you weren't hurt," Finnley said. "I was so afraid that—"

Mrs. T said sent the ball over to Finnley, who sent it back. And they were off. She shook her head and gave Finnley a look with a smile, though the smile was an act. "We only just met. You don't know me." Her words were focused and to the point. "I'm glad you came."

What happened to pretending they didn't know each other?

"What's going on?" Finnley didn't look at Mrs. T. as she returned the Ping-Pong ball.

She suddenly remembered she'd taken out her earpiece to talk to Caine. Where was it? What had she done with it? She was no good at this kind of thing. "What do you know about my father and what happened to him? Why am I here?"

"Calm down. Be patient. Act natural."

"Really?"

"Your questions will be answered soon enough."

"I'm doing my best to hold it together."

"You're doing wonderfully. You're strong and resilient and smart."

"How would you know?" Her challenging question brought a glance from the woman, who held her gaze for moment. Finnley couldn't read her. She was a blank slate. How did she do that? But more importantly, how in the world did Mrs. T know anything about her? "You must have been close to Dad."

The woman stiffened. "You should go. Find your friends."

"No. I'm not leaving until I get answers."

Mrs. T turned and stared across the room, and Finnley followed her gaze. Two men eyed them both, coming up behind Caine, who was heading in Finnley's direction. Caine suddenly turned. One of the men lifted something and pressed it against Caine's chest. He stiffened and collapsed.

"Caine!" Finnley started to rush forward, but Mrs. T grabbed her.

"No. We need to get out of here. They're after us." She pulled Finnley along with her. The woman had a stronger grip than Finnley would have imagined.

She appeared much older and thin and bony. Not someone with an iron grip. But once again, Finnley had judged this book by its cover.

"But my friend. You told me to go find my friends." Finnley wanted to help Caine.

But the men were closing in. Determined. Angry. And obviously dangerous. Where was Everly? Had they taken her out too? They were onto the Honor Protection team, and Finnley was on her own.

Except she wasn't. She was with Mrs. T, who, like Finnley's dad, was someone other than she seemed.

TWENTY

Caine gritted his teeth through the pain that felt like a million bees buzzing through his skin. He couldn't move.

And then...it was over.

His muscles responded to his brain.

Brett stood over him, holding his hand out. "Bro, are you okay?"

"No, I'm not okay! You try getting hit with 50,000 volts of electricity!" *Finnley! Finnley!* He got to his feet and grunted. "Where's Finnley?"

"Dude, let's get out of here. The ship doctor is on the way. Everyone is watching."

"He's okay," Brett said to the crowd watching.

"Yeah, I'm good. Just a..."

"He passed out. Too much medication."

"Stop, Brett. Just stop." He huffed and rushed out of the room down a wide corridor. Brett joined him. Caine communicated with Ayden and Everly. "Where is she?"

Everly approached. "She got away with Mrs. T. The two goons followed. Finnley took her communication out of her ear when you fought because you did the same. Caine, what were you thinking?"

"Not now, Everly. What about the tracker?"

Everly lifted a bag. "She left her purse behind."

"What?" Caine was about to lose it. "Guys, we have to get our act together and find her. We promised to protect her."

"Keep your voice down. Let's split up and search for her," Ayden said. "You see her pursuers, take them out."

"As in…"

"Subdue and cuff them. I've already notified security that we have a situation," Ayden said. "Let's go."

Caine took off but stumbled. Brett caught him and steadied him. "Are you sure you're okay?"

He grunted instead of responding, rushed across the deck to another exit and raced down the hallway. *We'll never find her in this big floating hotel.*

It was bigger than a hotel. It was a big floating convention center with something like twenty decks. Games. Theaters. Pools. A shopping mall. And rooms… Hundreds—thousands?—of rooms.

Oh Lord… Oh Lord…help me.

Adrenaline surged through him. Ayden had worked with the cruise ship security so they were allowed to bring their weapons. But Caine would have made a weapon out of anything at this moment.

All he needed was to get his hands on those two men.

He recognized them both from his encounters with them in town. One had been in the shadows watching the store and apartment. Caine had sparred with him but caught a glimpse of his face. The other had been in the apartment when Caine had fought him, wearing a mask, of course, but you never forget the eyes. Criminals can't hide their eyes.

He knew them both.

Wanted them both in cuffs.

Sweat beaded at his temples as he palmed his handgun under his jacket, trying to act normal so they wouldn't upset the cruise passengers. Let them enjoy their cruise while he tried to save Finnley's life.

If only he hadn't decided to have a serious conversation with her. Wrong time and wrong place. She'd still be wearing her earpiece if he hadn't had that conversation with her, wouldn't she?

"Where could they have gone? Where would the woman take her?" he said into his mic.

"I checked our rooms, and they aren't there. I'm going to see if I can learn Mrs. T's room, though I don't know the name she's using."

"I'm going to work with security and review the cameras' footage," Ayden said. "I'll find them. In the meantime, spread out and search. I'll let you know the minute I've learned where they are."

Caine continued walking the halls with no idea where Finnley could have gone. He'd let her down royally. He was the biggest jerk in the world. He had to make up for this. He had to make it right.

God, please help Finnley. Help her find answers and keep her safe. Please let us find and take down the criminal party here. I ask for Your protection and that no one gets hurt today.

His group wasn't necessarily there to take down criminals. Their most important job was to keep everyone safe. Ayden had significant connections to pull this off. Caine wouldn't let his siblings down. They were working hard for Finnley.

But right now, they were all part of a big failure if they didn't find her.

Would she ever forgive them? Caine found himself up on the top deck overlooking the ocean again. He walked fast and with purpose, searching for Finnley or Mrs. T. Or either of the two jerks or anyone else who looked like a jerk.

"Nothing. I've got nothing. Someone better tell me where she is," Caine said. "I'm heading back down, walking the halls. Ayden, anything?"

"Watching the footage now. Cruise security is on it too. In fact, they're demanding we stand down."

"What… What does that mean? I'm not going to stop looking for Finnley. Her life is in danger."

"They're requesting you turn your gun into them now. Head to security."

"Forget it."

"Caine!" Ayden shouted over his mic.

"Whatever. Just find her and tell me where she is."

"Got something. On the third level. Oh…that's not good."

"Tell me what's happening!"

Muted gunfire echoed behind Finnley.

She raced down another hallway. No one else was around. But someone was going to get hurt. She was sure of it. Could be her. She was going to get shot in the back.

Oh God, please don't let me get shot in the back.

Mrs. T was behind her, returning fire as they both ran. No one was supposed to have a gun on this cruise ship. But Mrs. T had found an unconscious security guard and relieved him of his gun for their protection. The bad guy had taken the security guard down, but not out completely. Finnley didn't know if she could forgive herself if someone else was killed because of all this mess with her father.

"There. Just there. Take a right," Mrs. T whispered loudly behind her. "We need to shake these guys."

Finnley stepped around the corner, but it was just another long hallway. Mrs. T quickly opened a door, shoved her inside and closed the door.

The woman pressed a finger against her lips, letting Finnley know to keep quiet, as if she didn't already know.

Mrs. T pressed her back against the door, gasping for breath, then she twisted, turned to press her head against the door to listen. "They passed us, but they could come back."

"This is your room?"

"No. I got to know a couple before coming over to you. Snatched their card after learning their room number."

"But why? Why would you do that? Who are you?"

Mrs. T half slid down the door.

"Wait. What's happening. Are you hurt?" The woman pushed from the door to head for a chair and then collapsed.

"You're shot. Tell me what to do." But Mrs. T's eyes were closed.

Finnley pressed her hands against the woman's side. *Oh, no! God, help me.* She grabbed a blanket and pressed it against the woman's side. She tried to find her cell, but it hit her that she'd lost her purse somewhere. Brilliant. She reached for the room phone and stretched the cord so she could continue to put pressure on the bleeding wound.

"Please help us. Someone's been shot! We need emergency medical services in stateroom C142."

There was suddenly noise outside.

The two men who'd been chasing them shot a hole in the door and then burst through. They must have heard Finnley calling for help through the door. She'd blown it.

"What do you want with me? I don't know anything that can help you!"

Mrs. T had fallen, and her hand still held the gun. Finnley slid her hand around the grip. It should be loaded and ready to fire. She couldn't be stupid and do nothing. These men had been after her from the beginning. Could they be the men who'd killed her father? They were probably the men who'd trapped her and Caine in her building and burned the place down with them inside. Nothing good could come from her trying to reason her way out of this. She had to act now.

Finnley would only get one chance at this before these men killed or abducted and tortured her for information they thought she had. This would be entirely different than the shooting range.

She calmed her breathing.

Calmed her pounding hurt.

Focused.

Caine's voice replayed in her head.

Aim for center mass.

Finnley whipped the gun out and fired two shots. Both men dropped to the ground. Finnley lifted her face to the ceiling and screamed. She'd just shot two men. Her heart was in her throat. The blood rushed from her head and dizziness overtook her.

Oh Lord...help me!

Someone entered the room. Vision blurred, she couldn't make out who it was. Fear choked her. Was he someone else that wanted kill her and Mrs. T? She aimed the gun at him, but her hands shook after she'd already shot two men.

"Whoa!" The man lifted his hands. "Finnley. It's me. Your dad's friend."

Greg Jones? What was he doing here? Dad hiked with him every year, and it made sense that he would know about the cruise too. She sagged with relief. "Greg! Oh, Greg…" She glanced at Mrs. T's wound. The bleeding looked like it had slowed, so she got to her feet. "I'm so glad you're here."

Greg took in the scene, his face in shock. "What happened?"

"Chaos. Total chaos," Finnley said. "What are you doing here?" And where was the medical help for Mrs. T…and for the two men she'd just shot?

She held the gun ready to use again in case Greg was yet another person who wasn't what he seemed. At this moment, she trusted no one.

He eyed the gun and was obviously aware she'd just shot two other people.

"I know it looks weird," he said.

"You have three minutes to explain yourself." Had she just said that? What was happening to her?

"Look. Listen. Okay." This guy was actually scared of her, while she held a gun at least. "Your father and I have been friends for years. You know that. He mentioned the cruise to me, so I knew about it. I was out of town, and when I returned, I learned that he'd died. Honestly, I decided to take the cruise to make sure you were okay. Just to kind of watch over you like he charged me to do if something ever happened to him. I should have just approached you."

Finnley wasn't sure how Greg had learned she was still taking the cruise, but his eyes filled with tears as he approached.

"I'm so, so sorry, Finnley. This never should have happened. I saw those two guys go after you, and I've been searching for you, and then I heard the gunshots. I'm glad I found you."

Finnley finally lowered the gun.

The man was sincere, and Dad had trusted him all these years. Maybe he could give her more answers. Maybe he knew what this was all about. She let him hug her, and she mourned with him. She grieved all over again.

Medical personnel rushed through the door. "The woman. She's still alive and bleeding. Please help her," Finnley said. "I don't know about the two men, if either of them is still alive."

Then Caine rushed in, his face pale but relieved. She'd never been happier to see anyone. She rushed to him. Caine pulled her into his arms, and Finnley let him. Her whole body shaking now, she pressed into him. He was someone she could trust. He'd proven that over and over again. He was even the one to protect Finnley's heart by pushing her away.

"Ma'am. We need to take you now. We've called a Life Flight helicopter." One of the medics leaned over Mrs. T.

"No, I need… Finnley." The voice was weak.

Finnley turned. Now conscious, Mrs. T was reaching for her. "Finnley, listen to me."

She moved in closer. This woman had answers for her.

"You need to go so they can treat you. I'll come talk to you in the hospital."

"In case I don't make it, I need you to know that my real name is Kathryn Jacobs. I know it's hard to understand right now, but I'm your mother."

TWENTY-ONE

Caine held Finnley close as they moved out into the hallway and watched the paramedics rush her *mother* through the door. He felt the shock of that news with her and thought he might actually be holding her up. He wasn't sure if she'd be able to stand if he let go. Three cruise ship security officers entered the room and looked at the two men on the floor.

Finnley had a lot to explain. Ayden came into the room too, with a serious take-charge attitude. Caine had never appreciated his brother more. He'd founded Honor Protection Specialists and had all the connections and kept them working and on good terms with local agencies. That gift and skill set was obviously playing out here.

Caine joined Finnley as she was ushered to another level and room, where the security took her statement. She was cautioned that local law enforcement—either the Coast Guard or Seattle Police Harbor Patrol, and potentially the FBI—would also talk to her.

The stateroom was now a crime scene, and the original occupants would be moved to another cabin.

Caine suspected that all Finnley wanted was answers. Greg might have them, but it was Mrs. T—Kathryn—who would share the most. If she survived.

He suspected Finnley's biggest questions had now shifted to just one—why had her mother abandoned her all those years ago? Caine held Finnley's hand through it all, but he was at a loss to offer her the comfort and support she truly needed. He had no idea what that was.

Everly and Brett hung back, but Ayden was right there in the middle. He approached Caine and leaned in close. "I've arranged for transportation off the cruise ship. Finnley wants to see her mother."

"I'm going too."

"I never doubted that. But she needs to get there and ask her questions before federal agents show up and shut the woman down."

Caine eyed Ayden. "What agency?"

"We'll see who shows up. Just keep an eye on Finnley. I hope this is over and Finnley is safe, but I can't be sure. She could still be in danger."

"Got it."

"Caine, watch your back."

"Always."

After everything they'd been through together, everything coming down on Finnley and their shifting relationship, Caine felt more like a hired protector. Finnley was distant, and that was just fine with him. It would keep him focused, except for the fact that his heart was breaking for Finnley right now.

He felt her pain intimately.

He recognized this for what it was. He had been here before. Though Caine resolved never to fall in love, he was mostly definitely falling in love with Finnley. She had distanced herself, closed herself off—understandably—but he felt the rift between them, and his heart was in pain.

Was he always destined to be a loser at love?

Still, now wasn't the time for these thoughts. He had to be there for her—whether he was in love with her or not. He couldn't give up on her or on them, but he understood that she wasn't in a place to think about him in these terms. If he got the chance, he would offer to be there to help rebuild her life—whatever that life looked like.

Finally, the helicopter arrived and transported the injured to the nearest major hospital, where they waited for Kathryn to come out of surgery. When the physician came looking for Finnley in the waiting room, he guessed it must have felt surreal to answer the doctor's questions.

"Are you the daughter?"

"Yes. How is she?"

"We removed the bullet. She's lost a lot of blood, but she should heal up and be fine. All her vitals are good and strong. Someone will come and get you when she's out of recovery and in her own room."

"Thank you." Finnley turned and moved to stare out the window.

To Caine, she looked completely lost in this world where she'd lost her father and now had a mother. She said nothing to him, but now and then she reached for his hand, and he knew she was counting on him.

Now more than ever.

Finally, she was allowed in Kathryn's room. The woman was sleeping. IVs were connected to her arms and a nasal cannula delivered supplemental oxygen. Two hours after Finnley and Caine arrived in her room, she finally woke up.

Caine nudged Finnley, who glanced up at her mother.

"You...you're awake." Finnley sounded exhausted.

"You're here." Kathryn blinked back tears. "I wasn't sure I would see you again."

"Of course. Why wouldn't I be here?"

"I guess you have a lot of questions."

Finnley moved closer. "And you have the answers."

Caine had a feeling that Finnley would be here even if Kathryn had no answers. This was her mother—if the woman could be believed.

"I'm just going to give you privacy," he said.

"No, Caine. Please stay." Finnley looked at him, her eyes pleading. And how could he say no to her? That thought startled him. Scared him.

"Okay. I'm going to stand at the door, though." *To make sure no one bursts in with guns. No one comes in to try to harm you again.*

The woman before Finnley had been so strong earlier, protected Finnley, but now she appeared weak and helpless. She'd just had surgery to remove a bullet, so of course she would look that way.

Finnley thought that she could see the resemblance in her dark eyes. Or maybe that was wishful thinking.

When she'd heard those words "I'm your mother," Finnley might have dropped to her knees if Caine hadn't been there to support her both physically and emotionally. The words continued to reverberate through her as she tried to comprehend. Her first thoughts were that the woman was lying, but in the deepest part of her, she knew those words to be true. She recognized something of herself in the woman's face, and she felt the love coming from her in waves.

But why? Why had she kept her identity from Finnley? She'd come to the shop every few months. She could have told her. All these years…

"Okay, Kathryn." She simply couldn't bring herself to call this woman Mom. Not yet. "I'm here. So tell me everything. Tell me why you stayed away all these years if you're really my mother."

"I'm trying to figure out how much is safe to tell you. So much of it is confidential."

"So you were a spy," Finnley said. The room tilted a little. Finnley had to hold it together. She had to hear this whole story. She'd waited so long to learn the truth. "Which agency did you work for?"

A small, painful smile came to her lips. "Your father and I worked together."

So her father had been a spy too. Finnley moved to lean against the wall. Of course. Now it was all making sense. But why was he killed? Finnley held the tears back.

"We shouldn't have…but we secretly got married. Having any kind of relationship was frowned upon. Getting married? I would have been fired on the spot. Not your father, though. That was years ago. I know things are different now. But I was caught up in the middle of a covert operation."

Kathryn stared at her hands.

"I had to go back and forth overseas, working undercover for a VIP. Then I found out I was pregnant."

The way she said the words nearly gutted Finnley. Her mother hadn't wanted her? "Was that such a bad thing?" Finnley almost scoffed.

"No, no!" Kathryn's eyes teared up. "Of course, I wanted you. But if my cover was blown…I would've been killed. You would have died too. So I hid the pregnancy as long as I could. I didn't show much." She closed her eyes. "And then… you came early and were premature."

For so long, Finnley had wanted to know more about her mother. Her father hadn't wanted to talk about her. Finnley had always thought it was simply too painful for him. Now, hearing her mother talk about being pregnant with her overwhelmed her. Unshed tears burned in her throat.

"So me coming early worked to your advantage." Finnley was crying now too. She couldn't watch this woman cry and not shed tears.

"Frank… He was close to retirement age for the agency, so he took it, and he took you. Cared for you. He opened the shop."

The shop was all about hiding Finnley in a remote small

town and working in an unlikely place. Finnley pressed her hand against her heart.

"How do you explain his secret office? The storage unit? He didn't seem to be retired to me. If he was retired, why did someone kill him?" *Just stop talking, Finnley!*

"It's complicated," Kathryn said.

Complicated? Did this woman even hear herself? Didn't she realize what Finnley had been through, seeing her father's body? Discovering he was someone else entirely?

"I need to know everything you can tell me. I need to know why Dad was killed so many years after he retired. And why you never once told me who you were. You came into the shop, and you never said, 'Oh, by the way, Finnley, I'm your mother.'"

There. She'd said it. And she wouldn't leave without all the answers.

"I simply couldn't tell you, Finnley. For your own protection and ours. Your father and I were in the worst kind of situation. I was working undercover but learned of treasonous activity committed by a VIP that shall go unnamed. I was afraid for my life. For yours and Frank's. I was being followed. My superior died in an 'accident' after I spoke to him privately before even filing a report. I knew as soon as I was reassigned that someone in the higher echelons realized what I had learned. I had to tread very carefully."

"Why didn't you just tell someone else at the government agency you worked for? Isn't that the whole reason to spy? To learn of treasonous activity?"

"Because Frank cautioned me against sharing anything. I'm not sure how to tell you without saying too much."

"Think about it this way," Finnley said. "I have been in danger, attacked, shot at, you name it, before I even knew anything at all. So it doesn't matter how much or how little I know."

Kathryn—Mom—looked at her long and hard and subtly

nodded. "Fair enough." She blew out a breath. "This VIP I mentioned... Frank feared that our superiors could be connected or beholden to him. For a time, I felt like the walking dead. That someone could silence me forever at any moment. I was...dispensable. Working for the government as an operative is a very complex, nuanced operation."

"In other words, you didn't know who you could trust with the information. You feared even your agency was compromised."

"Yes. That's it exactly. Our lives were in danger. So Frank made a plan. He collected the information and claimed he would share it once it was safe to do so. Though more than two decades went by after he retired, he remained connected loosely. He was prepared to protect his family if it came to that."

"So that explains the storage."

"No. That was all mine. Frank was an analyst. He wasn't a fan of guns, really."

Weird that he had a key and the storage was in his name, but the guns belonged to Mom. Weird that Finnley now felt comfortable referring to Kathryn as Mom. This was just so strange... She struggled to wrap her mind around it all.

"Why didn't you just resign?"

"I did, but that didn't mean I was safe. I had to disappear completely. Even so, someone was always watching, so I couldn't come to you. I couldn't claim you as my daughter. They would use you against me. I thank God that they never caught on to my connection to Frank. He was able to keep you safe. About five years ago, you'd finished college, and I started feeling things out. I visited the store. Then six months later, I popped in again. Over time, I came back more frequently, testing the waters, so to speak. Testing the safety."

Finnley shook her head. "Why tell me now, then? Are you still being watched?"

Kathryn pursed her lips and nodded. "Obviously. Once you

leave this hospital, never come back. Don't search for me or try to contact me."

Mom, I only just found you.

"What was the cruise about? Why insist I come? Why did Dad buy tickets?"

"We were all going to be together on the cruise. He was going to transmit the information to a high-ranking government official anonymously. We hoped we could finally be free to be together."

"I don't understand. Would it even matter all these years later?"

"Treasonous activity between a government official and a foreign country. Yes. It matters, especially if that person is still working in the government. But Frank believed we were out of danger now because I thought… I thought I wasn't being watched anymore. Finally. Years ago, it was easier to create a new identity than it is now. I've been living as Mrs. Tomlinson for so long, I almost forgot I was a spy. And I believed others had forgotten me. I erroneously believed that I was free and clear. Frank and I were making plans to finally be together. We planned to see each other on the cruise and meet as if for the first time. Build our family from there."

"But someone got to him before he could transmit the data," Finnley said.

"Or *because* he sent it. We were wrong to think that they were no longer watching." Kathryn swiped at her eyes and then closed them. She lay still, almost as if dead. The heart monitor still beat rapidly, so the woman—her mother—was still alive, but definitely stressed. Scared? She glanced at Caine, whose demeanor had clearly shifted into one of intimidation and protection. His cell rang and he glanced at her then gestured that he needed to take the call. She nodded. Then he stepped out of the room.

She and Caine were both in lethal danger by mere proximity to her mother.

Danger is my birthright. She almost laughed at the crazy thought.

They weren't out of this yet.

Kathryn opened her eyes. "Someone came to make him pay. The thing is, no one should have been able to know where the data was transmitted from. We should have been in the clear."

Finnley sat on the edge of the bed, anger and grief twisting her up inside. She had no more words. This was all just too much to take in. This information was in complete contrast to the life she'd lived.

Kathryn—Mom—pressed her hand against Finnley's. "Do you understand now that I stayed away because I love you?"

Okay. That was it. Finnley closed the distance and hugged her mother. The woman was either a really good liar and actress, or she was telling the truth. She hugged her hard and tight, and just as she suspected, the fragile-looking woman felt strong and tough.

Greg walked in, surprising Finnley, and she released her mother.

Where was Caine?

He dipped his head. "Finnley."

What is he doing here? "Kathryn, have you met Greg?" Did her mother know the man had come on the cruise too? Had come to try to save Finnley from the two gunmen, so he said. She wasn't sure where Greg was when Kathryn confessed she was Finnley's mother. She wasn't sure how much to say in front of him.

Kathryn eyed him with a warm smile, but wariness lurked in her gaze. "It's nice to meet you."

He glanced between Kathryn and Finnley. "I owe you an explanation."

"What are you talking about?" Finnley asked.

Greg came around the bed to stand near Finnley. "Again, I'm so sorry about your father."

With the story her mother had just shared and Greg's strange behavior, Finnley started to step away. She wanted to hit the call button. Wanted to grab her cell and call Caine, surprised he hadn't returned already. Or maybe he trusted Greg so hadn't stopped him.

Greg grabbed the back of her neck and squeezed it like a vise. "Careful now. I have a pin pressed against your neck. One prick, and poison will enter your bloodstream. You don't know anything. I've determined that. But if I let her keep talking, you might learn too much."

Kathryn stared in horror and in anger. Finnley's gaze locked with her mother's.

Tell me what to do, Mom? You're the spy. Tell me.

"Who are you?" Finnley asked, stalling. Hoping Caine or someone would come save them. Because a pinprick against her neck was going to be hard to escape.

She stood very still.

"As I said, I owe you an explanation. I was a plant. I played the role of close friend to find out if your father had intel that could be considered a threat. If I found anything out, I was supposed to make sure that your father didn't expose possible secrets he learned decades ago. I don't know what the intel was that was so important. I don't care. All I know is that my assignment came from the top man."

"Finnley…" Kathryn tried to sit up. "He—"

"Over time," Greg interrupted, "I became a genuine friend to Frank. We were friends for a long time. Please believe me, Finnley. But Frank sent the intel that I was supposed to stop. I had to do damage control or I'd be a dead man too."

Finnley tried to keep her voice even and steady, again stalling so help could come, if it was even coming. "What agency hired you to do this?" she asked.

"I used to work for a lesser-known subagency within the DOD, gathering intelligence. DIA—Defense Intelligence Agency. Same as Kathryn and Frank." He stared at Finnley's mother. "But I work alone now, for special operations."

Why would the top man try to bury this intelligence? Unless...the top man is connected to the traitor or actually *is* the traitor. Kathryn tried to slide out of the bed, but she wasn't able. "Let her go. Just let her go, I beg you."

"Begging is always good. I feel bad for what happened to Frank."

Finnley couldn't hold back. "I can't believe you killed my father. He was your friend!"

"Please, stop, Finnley." Kathryn's expressive eyes held a warning.

Finnley could be signing her death certificate if she said too much. But she understood now. She got it. Greg had killed her father.

"You said you were his friend. It's all lies. And who were those two men that I shot. They've been trying to get to me. Tried to kill me. Did you send someone to spy on me at the apartment?"

"Yes. I sent someone to watch you, to take you out and make it look like an accident. Or make it look like you killed yourself like your father, but you hired protection, which complicated it a little. The men on the cruise were there to take you and Kathryn—your mother—out. But you know the old saying—you want something done right, you gotta do it yourself. So here I am." He had a tight grip on her neck, and she expected to die at any moment. But she would learn the truth first.

"Except I find it harder to do this myself than I thought. I guess I've grown soft in my old age. I'll give you and your boyfriend a head start, Finnley. Go on and get out of here." He suddenly squeezed her neck tighter. "But remember this moment. Remember that I can get to you and kill you before you even know what hit you. I'll kill your friend first, though, so you'll know that I'm coming."

Terror swept over her. She fought to breathe.

Where was Caine anyway? Had Greg done something to Caine? Greg released her neck, and she stepped back, rubbing her neck. She'd been so close to death.

Greg lifted a pillow. "Get out of here now, or I'll end you here." He stepped toward her mother, obviously planning to smother her with the pillow.

"What are you doing? You can't do that!" Finnley started for him.

Greg suddenly rocked back and stiffened. He fell on his side, still stiff.

Caine stood in the doorway holding a Taser that had shot barbs across the room.

"Caine!" She gasped. Tears welled in her eyes. "Mom…" Finnley hugged her mother. It felt good and right to call her Mom now. The woman had risked so much.

Caine knelt next to the man and cuffed him. Two men in suits stepped into the room and took Greg. Finnley wasn't even sure that was his real name. She wasn't sure who the two men were. They looked like federal agents. She glanced at her mother. What did this mean for her?

Mom opened her eyes. "It's over now. Finally, over."

"How do you know, Mom? Your operation was so clandestine, so dangerous, how do you know that someone else is not out there looking for you or watching you?"

Her mother smiled, tears leaking down her face. She simply pointed.

On the widescreen secured to the wall, a breaking news

story played. "Retired General James Wilford, Secretary of Defense, has been charged with treason."

The top guy.

"Your father... He sent the information, after all."

Finnley could hardly believe that her parents had played a role in taking down such a traitor to the country. Now she fully understood why they were terrified. She could only guess that he must have been trading military secrets.

"I need some fresh air." Finnley raced out of the room, down the hall and stairs and burst out the doors. The wind gusted, clouds moved in, and a light mist saturated the area. She walked down the sidewalk.

She needed time to process everything, but it was so much, it was going to take a long time. She couldn't abandon the mother she'd found and wasn't sure if she was angry with her or could forgive her. Had she even done anything wrong? All she knew was that Kathryn was all Finnley had left.

"Finnley, wait." Caine caught up to her and walked behind her. "You shouldn't go out alone. We don't know that Greg is the last of them."

Finnley turned. Then again, this hazel-eyed protector, who had been there for her emotionally and physically, who had broken through the barriers of her heart... Maybe her mother wasn't all she had left.

Still, whether she had a future with this guy remained to be seen.

Caine looked her up and down. "Are you okay? Are you hurt anywhere?"

She covered her eyes.

I can't think about any of it right now.

TWENTY-TWO

Six months later

Fortunately, the small town of Emmons had not been rocked by press about spies and treason. That's because that information had been held close due to the nature of the classified intelligence secrets. That was totally fine with Finnley. She wanted to live her life in peace.

And because downtown Emmons was part of the historic district, funds were raised to rebuild the two buildings that had been destroyed in the fire. Finnley planned to restock her father's store, but she would hire someone to help run it. She wasn't sure she could live over the place, though. And the apartment, if one was built, wouldn't be her old apartment that she'd shared with her dad.

She still struggled to get used to the idea that everything was gone. Everything. Her old life was gone. The life she'd known had been built on a lie. But she wouldn't throw away the chance to get to know her mother.

Kathryn had fully recovered from her bullet wound, and though she had to travel to DC on occasion to answer questions in a government probe, her mother planned to stick around and spend the rest of her life with Finnley. Greg was in prison while he waited for his trial for murdering her father as well as a list of other charges in connection to his work after leaving the DIA. The hired henchmen that she'd shot on the cruise were also facing charges.

Justice was being served, albeit slowly.

As for the sheriff's department, Finnley wouldn't hold her breath and wait for an official apology from the sheriff for not believing her sooner, but Detective Wilson was kind enough to offer one.

Finnley stepped into the small café down the street and out of the rain, and Mom followed, laughing. They sat at a small table in the corner and ordered lunch. There was so much Finnley wanted to say. Wanted to know. She had no idea where to start. Their lives were finally settling into a rhythm, and she was connecting with Mom, so maybe she could start to have a deep conversation with her mother—the former spy.

"I'm sorry you didn't get to spend time with Dad. I mean, he was your secret husband."

Mom reached across the table and pressed her hand over Finnley's. "We make our choices, Finnley, and then we pay the price or reap the rewards. But I have you with me here now. I wouldn't change the time I had with your father, because at the very least I had that time."

The waiter came and took their orders.

"And that brings me to a very important topic. I want to know what happened to the brave woman who saved my life?"

"What's that?"

"Seems to me you're in love with a certain bodyguard."

"Oh, that."

"You've been pushing him away because you're scared."

"I…just found you. I need time with you. I don't even know who I am. I'm not…"

"So many excuses. Not that you're asking for my advice—I certainly haven't earned that right—but don't waste time with excuses. You love him. He loves you."

"My heart's been broken twice now."

"Would you really say no to a chance at a lasting love? Life is short. Believe me, I know. Please don't throw away this chance."

"I'll think about it. Everly told me they've invited you to be a consultant for them."

Mom took a sip of her tea. "Yes. I'm going to turn them down. They're good people. I was in the kitchen at their headquarters and saw the scripture on the wall. *'Do not be afraid; only believe.'* Mark 5:36." Her mother held her gaze as if needing confirmation.

"Yes, that's the one." Wow. Her mother was good at dropping subtle hints. And it was working. Finnley suspected God was trying to tell her to stop being afraid of getting hurt, of her future, and to have a little faith. She loved this woman, her mother, so much now after learning that she was not only alive, but she was back in her life. "What will you do, then?"

"I don't know. Maybe I'll open a florist shop. I've been thinking about creating beauty that others can enjoy. I want to grow flowers and make bouquets. Maybe I'll go to target practice now and then."

"Take me with you. Caine taught me how to shoot. I… I like it. I don't like hurting people, but I liked being able to protect myself."

"And you saved both our lives when you shot those men, Finnley. Don't ever regret what you did." Mom snapped her fingers. "I know. I could purchase some space here in town for a studio and teach self-defense for fun and getting in shape."

Finnley nearly lost her tea. "What? You're joking, right?"

"I'm not. I kind of like the idea. Or maybe just basic self-defense for ladies. How does that sound?"

"It sounds good, Mom." Finnley liked calling her *Mom*.

Her mother sipped tea, lifted her gaze to something out the window over Finnley's shoulder and got a knowing look on her face. Finnley glanced over her shoulder to see.

Mom leaned forward. "Finnley, don't let another minute pass without telling him how you feel. I'm going to go for a walk and get some fresh air. Maybe I'll look around to see where I'd like to lease my studio here in Emmons. I'll be back later." Mom patted her hand and then got up and left.

"But wait. You already ordered."

"It'll be here when I get back," Mom called over her shoulder. As she passed Caine, she whispered something in his ear and then exited.

Caine's smile was tenuous as he approached her. She got that her mother had set this up. She and Cain had seen each other on and off over the last few months as they worked through closing the investigation, and Caine had stopped by now and then to help with some of the renovations to her shop. The whole time, they danced around what they really wanted with each other.

She'd spent so much time pushing him away, and he'd done the same. It seemed neither of them knew how to reconnect or take that next step.

"May I sit down?" he asked. Yep. Nervous. But still too-good-looking-for-his-own-good.

"Yes, of course. What are you doing here? I mean… I'm glad to see you, Caine. It's a surprise, that's all."

He sat and looked at her, his hazel eyes filled with emotion and fear. "Finnley…" Her name came out breathy.

She'd hurt him. Oh, she couldn't bear it any longer. "I'm in love with you, Caine. I have been for a long time, but I've been afraid of getting hurt, and now I see I've hurt the both of us." *Oh, please…please be in love with me too. Maybe she'd spoken too soon.*

He opened his mouth and stared at her, then he grinned. She loved his grin.

"Come here," she said.

Caine still appeared taken aback, and he stood and drew her close. "When did you become so take-charge?"

"What? You don't like it?"

"I love it." He pressed his lips against hers and kissed her so long and hard she had no doubt that he loved her.

Caine eased back. "In case you didn't know, I'm in love with you too, Finnley. Please be mine. I can't live another minute without you in my arms, by my side. I want to kiss you a thousand times every day. Finnley Wilbanks, will you spend the rest of your life with me? Would you be my wife?"

"Yes."

Finnley pulled him close and kissed him again and again, and somewhere in the background, she thought she heard her mother saying, "It's about time."

* * * * *

If you enjoyed Caine and Finnley's story,
be sure to check out the other books in the
Honor Protection Specialists series
by USA TODAY *bestselling author*
Elizabeth Goddard.
Available now from Love Inspired Suspense!

Dear Reader,

I hope you enjoyed this last installment of my Honor Protection Specialists series. I had a lot of fun writing it. I love spy stories and often wonder about what retired spies do with their lives—if they survive being a spy (Ha!)—and I hope I'll have the chance to write more stories along the same vein. I love writing stories about characters who've struggled in their past but overcome their fears and find the strength to face the future. It's often the future and the unknown can scare us the most.

It's my prayer that you live life to the fullest and follow God's plan for your life, and remember...

"Do not be afraid; only believe." —Mark 5:36

I love to hear from my readers. Please visit my website at ElizabethGoddard.com and subscribe to my newsletter to get book updates and learn about exciting new releases!

Many blessings,
Elizabeth Goddard

HARLEQUIN
Reader Service

Enjoyed your book?

Try the perfect subscription for Romance readers and get more great books like this delivered right to your door.

See why over 10+ million readers have tried Harlequin Reader Service.

Start with a Free Welcome Collection with free books and a gift—valued over $20.

Choose any series in print or ebook.
See website for details and order today:

TryReaderService.com/subscriptions

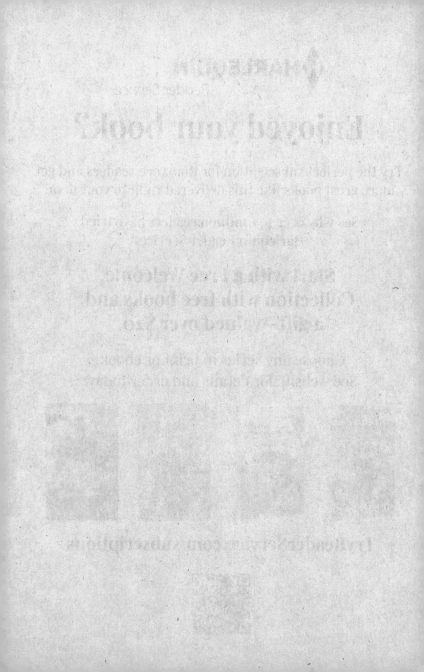